MW01132138

You'll Be Like Faye

you'll be like faye

J.C. BUCHANAN

ILLUSTRATED BY ANGELICA FERNANDEZ

Amethyst Publishing

Published by Amethyst Publishing

Text copyright ©2015 by J.C. Buchanan
Interior illustrations copyright ©2015 by Angelica Fernandez
All rights reserved.
ISBN 978-0692434758

www.jcbuchanan.com

Cover design by J.C. Buchanan & Iain MacKinnon
Typset in Garamond

Printed in the United States of America

To Mom and Dad
You guys are awesome!!

chapter one

just a dream

I jolted awake, breathing hard, and surveyed the room.

My bedroom stared back at me, peaceful, quiet. Outside, birds twittered, and downstairs, I heard rustling to suggest my mother was up, making her morning coffee. Everything was just as it always was. No car, no glass, no screams.

I had kicked all the blankets off during my nightmare, and as I came to grips with the real world, I realized I was cold. Shivering, I got out of bed and stretched, trying to rid myself of the terrible, reoccurring nightmare. After a minute of no success, a glance at the clock told me I was running late and I rushed to finish getting ready.

For some reason today, the scar that ran across my cheek seemed bolder. I bit my lip and put on an extra layer of lip gloss, hoping maybe it would draw attention away from the dreaded flaw. I wished Mom would let me wear real makeup—eye shadow or something. Anything to direct attention away from my cheek.

Maybe it was worse than normal, or maybe it was my imagination acting up, because I seemed to notice everything that I ordinarily did not today: the rough scratching of the carpet beneath my feet; the oldness, the beat-upness, the heaviness of my backpack as I slipped it across my shoulders; the feel of the smooth wooden railing as I ran down the stairs; the cold, tiled kitchen floor.

"Someone woke up late," Mom said, smiling at me. She sat at the kitchen table, drinking coffee— curly hair pulled into a bun, and in her pajamas; which meant she wasn't going into work today. That was happening more and more these days. I wondered why. I smiled back, still trying to shake the dream away. *It had seemed so realistic.*

"Morning, Mom," I said, wandering into the kitchen to find something to eat. Instead, I found my fifteen-year-old brother, Jack, stuffing his face full of chocolate cookies.

"Sup, Faye-Faye," he said when he saw me, and I sighed in annoyance, trying to ignore his pet name for me. His appearance was always horrible, but today, for some reason, it seemed worse. His blonde hair was messy and long, drooping and hiding his eyes. The printing on his t-shirt was so faded that I couldn't even tell what it had once said, and his jeans were torn so badly that it made me wonder how they stayed together. His tennis shoes, which had been new and shiny as of last week, were now scuffed up and caked in mud and other things from who-knows-where. He grinned mischievously, wiped the hair from his eyes, and slung his beat-up backpack over one shoulder. "What's up? Good dreams?"

Since when did my brother care whether or not I had good dreams? Naturally the nightmare flooded back to me. I stood frozen as the event replayed in my mind. After a second, I shook my head in attempt to clear my mind, and, at my wits' end, cried, "Aren't you late for your bus, Jack?"

He checked his shiny red watch, the only item he owned that he actually kept in good shape, and said nonchalantly, "Yep, five minutes and counting. Guess I'd better be going. See ya later, everybody!" —and he sauntered out, slamming the front door behind him.

Glad for some peace, I poured myself some cereal. Then the reason behind the sudden peace occurred to me.

"Stella's not up yet, is she?" I said.

"Nope, she's sound asleep," Mom sighed. "And she probably should be awake." Mom got up from the table slowly and made her way to the bottom of the stairs, still holding her coffee mug in one hand and mumbling something about why Stella couldn't just wake up to an alarm like normal kids.

"Stella!" she called up, tiredly.

"I'm awake," a muffled voice answered. A minute later, my eight-year-old sister appeared at the top of the stairs.

Stella was tall for her age and she knew it. Even though I was four years older than her, she stood almost at my height. Beyond that, though, we didn't look or think alike at all. Stella's bouncy blonde curls fell to her shoulders, her green eyes were bright and vibrant, and her skin was pale. Everything she wore had to have some form of glitter or sparkle on it, or she'd refuse to wear it. She couldn't be more different than me. My hair was a dull, straight brown, and my eyes were blue, and my left cheek was anything but smooth with the scar across it. I liked looking nice, but most of the time I ended up in jeans and a plain T-shirt.

Today, my sister tromped down the stairs in a sequin-covered skirt, neon pink shirt, her favorite blue headband, and sparkly tennis shoes that lit up in the dark. I began to wonder how such an outfit was acceptable for school when Mom instructed, "Stella, how many times do I have to tell you? That skirt is too wild for school. Go back upstairs and change right now."

Always stubborn, Stella pouted and held her ground, halfway down the stairs. "But I like this skirt."

"You can put it on when you get home, then." Mom was firm. "Do as I asked, please."

Stella crossed her arms. "Hmph!" She turned

and stomped back upstairs, her skirt catching the sunrays cascading in through the skylights. I sighed at my sister's antics. She was so picky when it came to clothes; when she was younger it was cute to see her dressed so wildly, but now it had gotten old. Stella *knew* Mom disapproved of her glittery clothing choices, but she still chose to wear them every morning and make a big deal out of it. Sighing, I hurried to finish my breakfast.

Minutes later, I threw on my backpack and laced up my shoes. "Do I look okay, Mom?"

She kissed the top of my head. "You look great, sweet. Have a good day!"

"You too," I echoed, and then I left. I shut the front door, careful not to slam, and raced down the steps of the walkway. Down the long driveway, past a few houses, and then to the bus stop. The whole way, I traced my finger across the scar, hoping it didn't stand out as much as I feared it did.

There was one person at the bus stop already. She had wild red hair, and bright-purple glasses framed her eyes. Her neon pink shirt and sequined coat reminded me of Stella. I grinned and ran to meet her, right as she ran to greet me.

"Faye!" cried Ellie Anderson, my best friend. "How are you? I haven't seen you in…in…in like twelve hours!"

I giggled, then my hand went instinctively to my face. "Do I look okay?"

"You look horrible, Faye." Then she elbowed me. "You look great! What, have I become your personal advisor?"

"Ellie," I laughed, "you've always been my personal advisor."

We both giggled. It felt good to laugh with her. The morning was cold and snow covered the ground. Above, puffy white clouds floated in an otherwise clear-blue sky. We discussed random things for a few minutes before the bus pulled up, ready to bring us into another long day of seventh grade.

•　　•　　•　　•

The day went by in the usual order; Ellie shared some of my classes, but not all of them. I eagerly anticipated lunchtime, when the three of us—Logan, Ellie, and me—could really spend time together.

At lunchtime, I pulled out my sandwich and Ellie, watching me, synchronized her moves with mine so we bit down at the same time. I laughed. Ellie swallowed, then she said, "I can't wait till summer break."

"Me neither."

Neither of us cared that it was a bit early to already be anticipating the last day of school. "We need better ways to pass the time."

Ellie nodded in agreement, but before she could speak, a boy my age wearing a ratty gray sweatshirt, ripped jeans, and black winter gloves approached the table next to mine, interrupting.

"Announcement! I, the Mighty Logan Beck, am on the premises!"

He threw a lunch bag on the table, pulled out the chair with much effort, and sat down abruptly. Recently he had developed the notion that wearing gloves in any environment made him look cool, and now, never stepped out of the house without them. His hair was bleach-blonde and long: too long, was his opinion. He was trying to convince his mom to allow him to dye it blue because he hated its current color, but so far he had no luck.

"What do you think is more reasonable, my friends?" he continued on with his conversation. "Dying your hair blue, or dying your hair dark, dark, *dark* green?"

I raised my eyebrows.

"Are you serious, Logan?" Ellie asked.

"Why else would I ask?" he said.

Ellie considered the matter for a moment, and then offered, very seriously, "The truth is, Logan, that I believe that hot pink would fit you more."

"Ellie!" I said, snorting.

"Pink?" said Logan in disbelief. "*Pink* hair?"

"Why not?"

Logan responded with a scowl toward us, then brightened. "Guess what?"

Ellie and I waited for him to continue, which he did quickly. "I'm going skydiving."

Biting into my sandwich, I arched my eyebrows.
"Translation?"

"I'm going to make a garbage bag parachute and jump off my roof," Logan said proudly, crossing his arms and whipping the hair from his eyes.

"Logan," I groaned, "Be serious."

"Oh, I'm serious all right," he responded, leaning forward. "Don't you believe me, Ell? Tell ol' Faye I'm being serious."

"Yep, he's serious all right," Ellie said. "He's going to jump off his roof and break his legs. And arms." She shifted her attention back to Logan. "When you limp into school on crutches, don't blame me."

"Who said anything about crutches?" Logan scowled.

"That's what happens to people who jump off their roof," said Ellie.

"Besides," I added, "I know as well as you do that your parents will never let you."

Logan made a face at me. "I'll have a parachute, Faye. Parachutes make it safe."

"Whatever, Logan," I said.

"Don't blame me when you walk in with casts on both arms," Ellie said.

Logan continued glowering at her while he ate. "Fine, then. Let's go back to our original conversation. What color should I dye my hair?"

"Blonde," teased Ellie.

Logan stuck his tongue out at her. "But with

this I'm actually serious—I'm desperate. If I don't get a hair color change, I am going to legitimately die."

"Oh, that's so sad," said Ellie, pressing a hand to her heart in mock concern. "I can already see the headlines: 'Twelve-year-old boy dies from lack of blue hair.' Such a traumatic way to die, don't you think, Faye?"

"Totally," I said, playing along and using all my willpower to contain my laughter.

"You guys are mean," Logan said, half-heartedly. "Okay, maybe I won't legitimately die—"

"That's a relief," said Ellie.

"—but I will probably become depressed." Logan crossed his arms as if making an important point. "And miserable. How would you like a depressed, miserable dude for a friend?"

"I don't know," said Ellie, pretending to think it over. "It actually might be quite interesting."

"Knock it off, Ellie Anderson!" he responded, with a light punch to her arm.

Before they could start up again, I intervened. "Okay, guys, really. We're getting too worked up about a small thing." I directed my attention toward Logan. "How would we even be able to help you?"

He bit into his sandwich decisively. "Point taken. The Mighty Logan declares this conversation has been *terminated*!"

I exchanged eye rolls with Ellie, then finished my lunch, laughing inside about the weirdness of our conversations and wondering how Logan even knew a word like *terminated*.

•   •   •   •

After school, I came home and went upstairs to do homework; there was too much of it these days. I worked my way through the stacks of pages until I finally finished, around five o'clock. I walked downstairs right as Dad walked in the door, home from work. He hugged Stella and me, high-fived Jack (who had developed the notion he was too old for hugs), hugged Mom, then announced the family would be eating dinner out tonight.

I was thrilled, as was Stella, and we didn't even try to hide our excitement. Jack kept his cool: "What's the big deal? It's just dinner out!" but we ignored him, caught up in the job of putting on our gloves, hats, and scarves. "I can't wait!" Stella giggled, as if were some important, exciting event (which, in her mind, it was).

All bundled up, we climbed into the backseat of our red minivan. I buckled myself in next to Stella while Jack droned on about how he didn't get why we were so worked up over just a restaurant and that we should start behaving like adults by keeping our cool. Or something like that. I stopped listening around word two.

Soon we arrived at the restaurant, Koz's, and eagerly climbed out. I breathed in deeply, anticipating my upcoming meal: mashed potatoes, Koz's specialty. Stella and Jack often pestered me for getting the same thing over and over, but I couldn't help it. Those potatoes were just way too good to pass up.

We squeezed into a booth against a window. I slid all the way to the back so my cheek was less noticeable. Stella scrambled to the end across from me and pressed her nose to the glass. "I can see our car," she announced proudly.

Jack snorted. "So can I. Big deal."

"Jack, leave your sister alone," Dad warned.

After we ordered, Stella flipped through the pages in her children's menu until discovering a page of tic-tac-toe boards and thrust it at me. "Wanna play?"

"Of course." I crossed an 'X' in the top corner with my green crayon. After much debating and deciding, Stella pressed her blue 'O' in the middle. A minute later, I'd won the game. Without thinking, I absently won the next four games. Afterwards, I looked at Stella's disappointed face, then at the boards covered in my proud 'X's. I bit my lip, feeling guilty, and flipped through the activity booklet to a blank page, where I drew five more tic-tac-toe boards. Stella's face lit up; and this time, I carefully let her win every game.

When we finally ran out of space, our food still hadn't arrived, so Stella decided we should play Rock, Paper, Scissors. Having nothing else to do, I obliged.

Ten rounds later, there was still no sign of our food. My mind wandered and I found myself listening to Mom and Dad's conversation. They were talking about work. I tuned out and looked out the window.

Mom and Dad owned an architecture firm in the city. Dad drove in to the office every day, but Mom only worked part-time. The days she wasn't going into work, she worked from home; that's how much she loved her job. Dad loved his job, too, but since he owned the firm, it was required for him to go into work each day.

The restaurant was taking longer than normal today. Stella, who'd grown bored of doodling over her activities, was fidgeting in her seat. "Will it come already?"

"It has been long." Dad peered around. "I don't see anything yet."

"Well, it better soon," Jack said, crossing his arms. "I, for once, agree with Little Sis. It's been *so* long."

Stella grumbled, never noticing, or caring, what Jack's opinions were. "I'm so *hungry*," she complained, "and we've been *waiting—*"

"Stella May, you need to be patient," Mom told her sharply. "I didn't bring you here to listen to you whine."

Stella pouted and looked away, defiant.

"Aww, look at Little Sis!" said Jack sarcastically, the absence of food finally starting to mess with him. "Doesn't she look so cute when she's mad?"

"Stop!" said Stella.

"Jack," said Dad warningly.

Jack didn't say anything. He looked out the window for a minute, then back at us. "When will our food be here?"

"Jack, did you listen at all to the conversation I just had with Stel?" Mom cried.

"What conversation?" Jack faked innocence.

Before anyone had a chance to answer him, the food arrived. Finally. Unable to wait a minute longer, I helped myself and dug in.

As we ate, we discussed random things, events of the day, that sort of thing. Not having much to say, I pretended to be deeply interested in Stella's story of a conversation she'd had with a new girl at school. But the only thing I really picked up from Stella's well-detailed monologue was that the girl's name was Charlotte.

Afterwards, we stood up and stretched while Dad paid the bill, then we all walked to the exit, through the awful cold to the car, where we piled in and buckled, shivering. Stella, as always, found a new thing to complain about. "I really want an ice cream cone, though, Daddy! Please? Pretty please?"

"No," said Dad firmly, starting the car. Warm blasts of air came from the vents, and I took it in eagerly. Next to me, Stella pouted and crossed her arms. "But you *promised* we'd get ice cream!"

"I never promised," Dad responded. "I said maybe."

"But you got my hopes up," Stella pouted.

"But you got my hopes up," mimicked Jack.

"Jack, stop," Mom warned.

The rest of the ride was spent ignoring Stella's complaints and Jack's occasional teasing. I watched the dark landscape speed by, and soon, we were home.

Dad parked the car in the garage, and we all climbed out. As we walked in, Mom suddenly stopped, turned around, and groaned. "Faye, would you please go get the mail for me? I know it's dark…but I completely forgot earlier."

The night was cold and dark, but I could see the mailbox from here and the house lights illuminated most of the drive. "It's fine. I'll do it."

Shoving my hands deeper into my coat pockets, I shuffled through the snow to the mailbox at the end of the driveway. I opened it and retrieved the mail, and at the last minute noticed a bright green flyer wedged between the box and the flag. Holding the piles of envelopes in one hand, I grabbed the flyer with my free hand, slammed the metal door shut, and walked back up the driveway.

chapter two

a cleaning service,
only a cleaning service

"What's this?"

Shuffling through the mail, Dad had discovered the
flyer that had been wedged between the box and the
flag.

"I don't know." I was still discarding my
winter gear. "It was behind the flag. What is it?"

"An advertisement..." He scanned the flimsy,
wet paper. "For a cleaning service."

"A what?"

"Cleaning service," he murmured thoughtfully,
and tapped the page a few times as he thought.
Finally, he laid the ad down and said, "I've got to
find your mother," and scurried away.

I kicked my boots into the closet and slid
across the kitchen floor toward the pamphlet.

Does Your House Need Cleaning?

Call Brittney Ferry!

I will do all the dirty work
So YOU don't have to!
Vacuuming, Dusting, Mopping....
You name it, I'll clean it!

Prices are Negotiable.

Below was listed a phone number and email address for the assumed "Brittney Ferry." Was Dad actually considering this? Did this mean I would never have to clean my room again?

"What's this?" My brother, who loved to snoop into business that wasn't his, pushed in front of me and grabbed the paper. In one motion, he pushed his bangs back and scanned the whole thing. "A cleaning service! Sweet! Room cleaning's out the window!" As if demonstrating his point, he tossed the paper in the air. "Whoohoo…" His voice trailed off as he pounded upstairs and slammed his bedroom door behind him. I sighed, scooped the paper up from the floor, and then placed it safely back on the kitchen table.

•   •   •   •

"So…when do I get off duty for room cleanup?" Jack asked at dinner, a couple nights later. He squeezed a mountain of ketchup onto his burger, slapped the top bun on and bit in, glopping pasty tomato all over his face and hands. Not that he cared or even noticed; Jack had never used a napkin voluntarily in his life.

Mom and Dad exchanged glances. Stella asked, "What do you mean?"

"Jack, how did you know about that?" Dad said calmly.

"Dad," said Jack, with a challenging look. "It was *laying* on the kitchen table."

"Okay." Dad seemed flustered, as did Mom. She took a breath and looked at us. "Okay, Jack, fine. Yes, your father and I have given it much thought, and we decided we're going to hire her."

Jack pumped his fist in the air. "*What up*! Chores are out the window for me!"

"Wait!" said Stella, now befuddled. "What are you talking about?"

I felt bad that she was so confused. "Stella, we're getting a cleaning service."

Jack was still cheering. "Whoohoo, whoohoo, whoo—"

Mom sighed loudly and closed her eyes. "You're getting the wrong impression, Jack."

"She isn't here to clean up your junk," Dad said. "I don't think she's even doing regular housework; she's mostly doing the hard work, the work that your mother…um…isn't up for these days. Windows, mopping, et cetera."

"Come on!" Jack said. "This is *such* a disappointment!" His voice, however, told me that he was more interested in drawing attention to himself than feeling disappointed that he wasn't getting his room cleaned for him.

"Wait, did you say 'she'? How do you know it's a 'she'?" Stella asked.

"It was on the flyer, Stellie-Girl," said Jack smugly.

"Well, Jack's half right. It does say so on the paper, but I also did call the number today," Mom admitted sheepishly. "It's all arranged. Brittney Ferry is her name—the cleaning girl. She's coming next week."

Well, wasn't this sudden.

"So will she be here every day or what?" Jack asked Mom, sticking a French fry in his mouth.

"Mondays, Wednesdays, Fridays," Mom replied promptly. "One to four. She'll be here when you get home from school."

"Sweet!" said Jack. "So I get to watch her?"

"*Watch* her?" Dad repeated.

"Yeah, why not?" Jack said. "I want to see her work in progress."

Dad looked at Mom and she returned the gaze; they were both exasperated with Jack's smart comments.

"Why would you want to watch someone clean a kitchen?" Stella said slowly. "You're crazy."

Jack flashed another grin. "I know," he said.

•   •   •   •

I slept long and hard that night. And, thankfully, without any nightmares. I woke before my alarm, earlier than normal, and instead of rolling out of bed, I laid there for a little while, just thinking, about the previous day, about the cleaning service, about my friends.

Ellie and I had been best friends forever. Well, at least, since second grade. I had always lived here, in Forest Grove, but at the time, Ellie had just moved in down the street, and we were both at the neighborhood park. I was playing on the swings while Mom pushed the stroller around (Stella was only a baby still). Ellie had arrived at the park, and, upon seeing me, broke away from her mom and marched over to me. Always outspoken, Ellie stood impudently in front of my swing. She then smiled and said, "Hi! I'm Elisabeth Madilyn Anderson and I'm seven and I think we should be best friends forever. But only if you call me Ellie. 'Ellie' is just so much better than 'Elisabeth,' don't you think?"

Being seven and currently without a best friend, I leapt at the opportunity, responding that my name was Faye Violet Corcoran and I thought we should be best friends too. She'd come over to swing next to me, and we'd started to talk, a conversation that lasted for far too long, until Mom announced it was time to head back. Ellie shared her address, and I told her mine. We lived on the same street, about ten houses away from each other. We'd also discovered we'd attend the same school. I went home that day excited, and called her that night to talk more. We'd been fast friends ever since.

In fourth grade, a new kid named Logan Beck moved to the area and joined our school. During lunch his first day, he had spent most of the lunchhour wandering around the cafeteria before sitting down decidedly next to us. He took a gulp of soda, stuck a pretzel stick in his mouth, and proudly told us his name was Logan and asked us ours. Introductions were made, and this meeting eventually grew into a strange sort of friendship between us: at the very least, we sat together at lunch every day.

Only once did Ellie ask Logan if he had any friends who weren't girls. Never one to be embarrassed, he promptly replied that he had friends on his street, but since they didn't go to this school, he was more than happy to hang with us during school. Since Ellie and I were happy about it too—Logan was fun and had a great sense of humor—we didn't bring it up again.

Lying in bed, I smiled at the memories, and then made myself get moving.

I darted down the driveway to the bus stop with a spring in my step. I couldn't wait to tell Ellie about the cleaning service, even knowing Ellie's overdramatic tendencies.

As expected, Ellie's eyes grew wider and wider as I explained the situation. "You're getting a cleaning service?" she said, her voice full of awe. "Lucky!"

"Well," I began, trying to explain before she jumped to conclusions and got the wrong impression, but she interrupted before I could continue. "In other words, you're saying you're done cleaning your room and doing chores? For, like, an *eternity*?"

I sighed, but I wasn't mad. Ellie's other tendency was to get worked up over the tiniest things, but it was what made Ellie *Ellie*.

"No, not exactly, Ellie," I proceeded to explain, right as the bus rolled up. I finished my sentence as we climbed aboard and found our seats. "She's just doing, oh, I don't know—the bare housework. Mopping and stuff, I guess. I still have chores, and I still have to clean my room. Besides, she'll only be here three days a week."

Just like Stella, Ellie asked me, "It's a 'she'?" While waiting for me to answer, Ellie plopped her bag on the floor and turned, leaning against the bus window.

I explained. "It's a cleaning lady."

"Even awesomer," she breathed. "And it makes you even luckier. I mean, think about it, BFF. A lady is coming to your house to clean it." She said the last part slowly, as if maybe I wouldn't understand the full concept otherwise. Her eyes widened. "You'll be like rich people!"

I rolled my eyes good-naturedly. "Don't you think you're being a bit overdramatic?"

"No," she said plainly, then, "Wait till Logan hears!"

I joked, "We're telling Logan?"

"Of *course* we're telling Logan!" Ellie sputtered. "How could you ever dream of keeping something this big from him?"

"If it wasn't that big," I teased her.

"Faye!"

"I know," I giggled.

•   •   •   •

Over lunch, Logan was, to my surprise, deeply interested in the whole matter, though he didn't overdramatize it like Ellie. "That's really cool, Faye. And I'm speaking from experience here, we have a lady who comes to clean once a month."

Ellie gaped at him. "Really?"

"Yep," he said. "She's really good, too. No fair, though. I wish she would come three times a week! I'll have to ask my mom!"

"Yeah, Logan, then you'll be like Faye," Ellie piped up. I rolled my eyes.

"But why do you need a cleaning service?" Logan asked me. "And why now? Is your house like suddenly super messy? I mean, when Amelia started, it was because my mom had to go back to work."

"Well, my mom already works from home a lot." I looked at him, puzzled. "I actually don't know why. Our house isn't *that* dirty."

"Confusing," Ellie commented. "Well, let me know when you figure out the answers."

"I will," I said, slowly. "I will."

chapter three
meet miss ferry

The days flew by. Every day was school, and every day there was something to laugh about with Ellie and Logan at lunchtime, whether it was the bizarre type of sandwich Logan brought or a funny joke Ellie said. After school, there was always that long hour of homework, which I hated. Dinner, and then I hung out downstairs with my family, sometimes reading, sometimes doing yet more homework, occasionally playing a game with Stella, and sometimes Jack, if we could persuade him.

The following Monday morning, the day the service started, Mom explained, very carefully, how it'd work.

"She'll be here when you get home," Mom said. "We'll introduce you, but after that, why don't you go do your homework in your room? She might be doing work in the kitchen, and I don't want you to get in her way."

"Fine," I said as I rushed to get everything I needed, not mentioning I did it in my room most days anyways.

Mom glanced at the clock. "Goodness, Faye, you're almost late!" She gave me a kiss on the cheek as I started to run to the door. "Have a good day, sweet."

"You too," I said. I shut the door behind me and I was off. I was halfway to the bus stop before I realized that, yet again, Mom had been in her pajamas. That yet again, she was staying home from work.

I didn't have long to wonder over this, though, because Ellie, bright and enthusiastic as ever, was waiting for me on the bus. As soon as I sat down, she had a grip on my arm. "It—she's beginning today, right?"

I sighed. "Yes," I said, shaking her hand off. "You are correct."

"Ooh!" She practically squealed. "This is, like, so amazing!"

I had to laugh, at that. Sure, the whole thing was exciting, but the way Ellie acted made one think royalty was coming for dinner. "It's just a cleaning lady, Ellie."

"Yeah, but she's going to *clean* your *house!*" Ellie cried. "Like, in other words, you're done with chores? For, like, an eternity?" I laughed and shook my head. Nothing I said changed Ellie's thought process, so it wasn't even worth it to tell her again that I was still responsible for chores. Anyway, I knew it was most likely she kept repeating it only to get to me.

"You think I'm being silly," Ellie went on, "but I would do *anything* to be in your shoes."

I looked at her. "Maybe me and you should swap places, then."

I had been joking, but Ellie's eyes opened wide. "Hey! Now *there's* a great idea, my friend! We totally should!" She grabbed a fistful of her own vibrant red hair and compared it to my own dull, dark brown. "Our hair color's pretty close, Faye," she said seriously. "I might be able to pass for you."

I giggled. "You think?"

Ellie wasn't finished. "And we both have eyes that aren't brown," she continued, one fact I couldn't argue with (my eyes were blue and hers green). "Aha! You could wear my glasses!" Ellie pulled her purple, gemstone-embedded glasses from her face and shoved them on mine. "Ooh, now I can't see," she said, squinting at me in vain. "Unless you squint a lot and bump into everything, this won't work...Come on." Her voice was dead serious, but I couldn't keep my face straight as she took her glasses back. "There. Much, much, better. I still wish we could find a way to make your idea work, though..."

•   •   •   •

School finally ended after a long, tiring day. At our stop, I said goodbye to Ellie and started walking to my drive. It wasn't until I saw the unfamiliar car in my driveway that I remembered about the service.

My heart fluttered a bit, and I allowed myself a quick laugh at myself. Ellie really was rubbing off on me. Still, it was exciting, if not nice, to have some change, some difference in my life.

I went up the driveway, past the car. It was rusty and a faded blue.

As I reached our walkway up to the front door, I stopped, quickly pausing to look at our house, my home. I loved every bit of it: from the crooked shutters on Stella's window that Dad kept saying he needed to replace, to the nice, cream-colored siding and the deep blue of the roof shingles. My window faced north around the corner, but I could see the pink curtains framing Stella's window and the dark shades of Jack's.

After a pause, I ran up the steps into my house. In the kitchen, Mom was talking to Jack, who was playing some game on his iPod. There was no sign of our apparent new service anywhere.

"Hello, honey," Mom said as I dropped my bag on the floor and slid into the seat next to Jack.

"Hey," I replied. "First of all, I thought we had a cleaning service? And secondly, since when can Jack play games before homework?"

"None of your business," Jack retorted, without looking up. "You forget your big brother gets home before you and has more time. Has the thought crossed your mind that maybe I've already finished?"

I rolled my eyes and looked away, taking the chocolate chip cookie Mom offered me.

"In answer to your question, Faye," Mom said, "she's upstairs. I believe she's vacuuming bedrooms. We'll have a formal introduction when she comes down." Mom winked at me.

"Okay."

While Mom had apparently not been well enough to attend work, she had been feeling well enough to bake. The cookies were still warm from the oven, and the chocolate melted on my tongue as I bit in.

A few minutes later, I heard footsteps and turned around just as a young woman walked into the kitchen, set down a vacuum, and wiped her brow. The cleaning lady. She was much younger than I had expected, maybe nineteen or twenty. We took each other in. She scanned my new pink jeans to my sparkly sweater; her eyes finally traveled up to my cheek, and lingered for a moment. Our eyes met, and I broke the contact, studying her instead.

Her caramel-colored hair was pulled into a loose bun, held back by a pink headband. Her gray sweatshirt, faded and worn, covered a pink top. My gaze drifted down her ripped jeans to her scuffed-up tennis shoes, then back up to her kind face. Mascara framed her bright blue eyes—not unlike my own—but otherwise her face was makeup-free. She almost seemed familiar for a moment, but then the moment passed.

"Ah, Brittney!" Mom put an arm around me. "I'd like to introduce my daughter, Faye. Faye, this is Brittney Ferry."

"Hi," I said shyly. We shook hands; her grip was firm. "It's nice to meet you, *Faye*," she said, emphasizing my name. Her voice was gentle and clear, and she looked like she was choosing her words carefully. I half-smiled back. "You, too."

"Brittney," said Mom. "I'm sorry to have interrupted you. Do you have any questions so far?"

The visitor considered the matter for a moment, and then said, "Actually, I'm doing fine, Mrs. Corcoran."

"Well, thank you, Brittney."

"You're very welcome, Mrs. Corcoran." She smiled warmly at me, and then dragged the vacuum into my parents' bedroom, down the hall. After she'd left, Mom turned to me. "Why don't you get started on your homework?"

Jack was still at the counter, zeroed in on his iPod, but I decided to leave him alone. I grabbed my bag and tromped upstairs to my room.

My workload was less than usual. When I finished the last page, I slipped it into my folder and sighed gratefully, plopping back into my desk chair. Brittney was still downstairs, though I couldn't hear the vacuum. Remembering how excited she'd been, I decided to call Ellie. She would be dying to hear every last…boring…detail.

I didn't own a cell phone yet, but today, one of

the cordless phones was still in my room from a previous conversation with Ellie. I called her and she picked up right away.

Without even saying hi, she began the conversation. "FAYE! Tell me *everything*!"

I laughed. Downstairs, I heard the vacuum begin again, so I walked over and shut my bedroom door. Ellie continued: "Tell me every detail about this 'cleaning lady,' Faye. *Right. Now*!"

"More like cleaning *teenager*," I said. Okay, so I was maybe stretching the truth a bit, but nineteen-year-olds were still *teen*agers, right? True, I didn't know for sure she was nineteen—but it had to be close. "She's like, eighteen or nineteen or twenty or something."

"Ooooh!" Ellie replied, ever-fascinated. "What's her namey?"

"Namey?"

"Quit stalling, Faye! You know what I mean!"

"I do?"

"Stop!" she yelled in my ear. I pulled the phone away, laughing, then said, "It's Brittney."

"Mysterious!" commented Ellie. "And I said *every* detail. You forgot to mention her last name?"

"Ferry?" I guessed. "Yeah, it's Brittney Ferry."

"Extra mysterious," she said. "Okay, next subject. What's she doing now?"

I rolled my eyes. "Would you mind explaining why this is such a mystery to you? It's just a house cleaner."

"*Exactly*!" she said. "It's a house cleaner! You

never really know with house cleaners. Do you know that Logan's house cleaner was a ex-convict?"

"What in the world, Ellie?"

"Okay, maybe I made that up. It doesn't matter! Brittney's a different person! She's totally mysterious."

"You haven't even met her, Ellie."

"When you're a detective, you trust your instincts."

"And you're a detective?"

"Whatever, Faye!" she shouted in my ear. "Just tell me what's she's doing right now."

"I don't know, I'm in my room."

"Well, go look!"

"Whatever you say, Princess Ellie," I teased, leaving my room. I went onto the loft and leaned over the railing. I couldn't see Brittney, but I still heard the vacuum from the direction of the front room. "She's vacuuming," I whispered.

"Oh," whispered Ellie. "Why are you whispering?"

"I don't know, why are you whispering?"

"Cause you are."

I sighed, rolled my eyes, and laughed. "I'll tell you more at school tomorrow, okay?"

"What!" Ellie shrieked. "You're not going to tell me more now?"

"I'm going downstairs to see if Stel's home yet," I responded.

"So what? You're good at multitasking. You can talk and walk. Hey, that rhymed! Talk and—"

"And have Brittney overhear everything we're saying about her?" I interrupted.

Ellie was silent. "Okay, you do have a point there. Promise me you'll talk tomorrow!"

I sighed. "I promise."

"Good," Ellie brightened. "See you then!"

"See you," I echoed.

I hung up and walked downstairs, replacing the phone where it belonged.

Stella, whose bus arrived each afternoon at 3:45, had just gotten home and was in the kitchen, looking for something to eat, as always. "Hey," she said. "Did you meet Brittney?"

"Yeah, did you?"

"Uh-huh." She opened the fridge, surveyed the contents, and then slammed it. "There's nothing to eat."

"Cookies," I said, pointing to them.

She gave me a look. "Yeah, but I already had one and Mom said I can't have another."

I shrugged and went to look for a snack myself. After a minute, I grabbed an apple out of the fridge, rinsed it off, and took a bite. "There are apples, Stel."

"Well, I don't *like* apples."

"Suit yourself." Taking another bite, I walked around and into the family room, casually looking around for Brittney. Instead I found Jack, still on his iPod, sitting on the couch with his feet kicked up on the table. I sat beside him, loudly munching.

Without looking up, he said, "You aren't

supposed to be in here with food."

Oops. I scowled at him, though I doubted he saw it, and went to sit at the kitchen table, keeping within talking distance. After a minute, the unbelievable happened: Jack set down his iPod and looked at me. "So. Faye."

"So. Jack."

"What do you think of...you know?" He gestured towards the sound of the vacuum. "Brittney?"

I shrugged and took another bite. "She's nice."

"What'd Ellie say?"

"How'd you know——"

"You don't think I didn't hear you on the phone when you were on the loft?"

"Fine." I shrugged. "Nothing more than normal. She's so excited, it's so mysterious, et cetera, et cetera, et cetera."

Jack scoffed. "Mysterious? What's mysterious about a cleaning service?"

I gave him a look. "Nothing, Jack. But you know Ell—if I told her Stella painted her nails sparkles she would say it's mysterious."

Jack just lifted his eyebrows, and then retrieved his iPod.

I wouldn't be hearing from him the rest of the day. There goes the idea of an actual conversation that lasted longer than two minutes. I tossed my core in the garbage and left.

•   •   •   •

Brittney was in the foyer, vacuuming. I wandered over and leaned up against the wall, to watch her work for a minute. I almost laughed, remembering Jack's proclamation about how much he wanted to watch her "work in progress." Right, like that had happened. His electronic device was the only thing that had captured his attention since he walked in from school.

I noticed Brittney's diligence, her carefulness, her attentiveness to detail. Mom and Dad were definitely paying her for a job well done.

She eventually looked up, caught me watching her, and smiled warmly. I returned and impulsively made an about-face to relieve us both from a potential awkward moment.

She turned off the vacuum and wound up the cord.

"You don't have to leave," she assured in a tone that kind and comfortable, as if we'd been friends for years. Finished with the vacuum, she dug through her bucket of supplies until she found a rag and window cleaner. Her hand moved with calm, rhythmic strokes as she wiped down the living room picture window. Most likely curious if I was still silently standing in the room watching her, she smiled over her shoulder toward me.

"Um…" I stammered, unsure what to do or say.

"Faye, right?" She began putting away her rags, sprays, and other supplies as she talked. Mom had said she would be here one to four o'clock, and according to the wall clock, it was 3:53 now.

I nodded, slowly.

"You're.... twelve?" she guessed.

"Twelve and a half," I responded. Okay, so maybe I was a little too old to refer to half ages, but...whatever.

"Well," Brittney was saying, "I'm twenty-two and a half. So I guess we both have birthdays to look forward to sooner than later, huh?"

Too bad I'd already hung up with Ellie. She'd be all over this.

I followed her as she put away the vacuum. I was surprised she was using ours, rather than her own. "My parents let you use ours?"

She laughed lightly. "Yes, in fact. They're very...kind people." She seemed uncomfortable a second, but maybe I imagined it. She switched the subject. "So, you're the middle child."

"Yep." I leaned against the countertop. "Stella's eight and Jack's fifteen." Sort of an afterthought, I asked, "Do you have any siblings?"

Brittney suddenly turned away and inhaled sharply, like she hadn't been expecting the question, and quickly busied herself re-packing stuff that was already put away. After a long pause, she said, "No," and seemed very uncomfortable about it. "Um...okay." I didn't want to push further, but I was instantly curious about her reluctance and

uneasiness.

Brittney, still tense at my past question, glanced at her wrist. I noticed for the first time the piece of junk strapped there. It had, at one point, probably been a nice watch. Now, the rust, the fading, and the overall horrible condition of the watch made me wonder if it still operated. Apparently, it did, because Brittney looked up and said, "Well, it's four."

"Thank you!" I hadn't notice Mom creep up on us.

"Anything else you need done?" Brittney asked.

"You were great, Brittney. Thank you so much," Mom said, putting an envelope into Brittney's hand.

Brittney nodded gratefully as she slipped on her old, ragged coat and tucked the envelope in the pocket.

"You've done a fine job, Brittney," Mom reassured her again. "We'll see you Wednesday."

The front door slammed behind her. I looked around our house, nice and clean.

"Well, Faye." Worn-out and tired Mom was back. "What do you think?"

"Of what?"

"Everything."

I shrugged. "Brittney's nice. And the house is clean."

Mom laughed. "It most certainly is! She did a great job."

I nodded in agreement, though my mind was still whirring with questions.

chapter four

what's the matter with mom?

February came to a mostly uneventful end. But as was usual this time of year, spring itself still seemed reluctant to show up. Snow covered the ground, and the weather was chilly, if not bitter. Even though a few snow days still made some appearances in the first weeks of March, Brittney never failed to show up for work. Every time I thought for sure the snow was too heavy, the roads too icy, the wind too whipping, my thoughts proved false when I'd come home from school and that rusty old excuse for a car would be parked in my driveway.

One particular day, I woke up to see snow sleeting down outside my window, so foggy I couldn't even see across the yard to the house next door. I didn't even have to ask Mom to know that school had been canceled.

"Snow day, snow day, we get a snow day," sang Stella from the living room. I tromped downstairs, my blanket still wrapped around me.

I poured myself a bowl of cereal and ate slowly, savoring each bite, each lazy minute of not having to rush around or get ready for school. I was nearly done before Jack lumbered down the stairs in his pajamas. "When's school?"

"It's a snow day, dummy," Stella said.

"Stella, do not use that language," Mom chastised.

"Sorry," she mumbled.

"It's fine," Jack said. He was in a good mood this morning, but that wasn't unusual. He was normally in a good mood on snow days. He poured a bowl of cereal, spilling both cereal and milk on the counter and floor in the process.

I left the scene to get dressed before the chaos got any worse.

• • • •

Ellie called around ten, no surprise there. We talked for a few minutes about snow day and school, that sort of stuff, and then Ellie brought up Brittney. Of course.

"So, is Brittney at your place today?"

"Um, she doesn't get here for a few hours,

Ellie, and I don't even know if she'll be able to come if the storm gets worse."

"Right," Ellie said. "Wouldn't want to lose your reliable cleaning lady to a snowstorm."

"Ellie!" I gasped.

"I know, Faye, I was being funny, okay?" She grumbled something under her breath about me having no sense of humor, but I knew that was just her own sense of humor playing with me. I rolled my eyes.

"Well, I got to go," she said. "I would ask if I could come by, you know, maybe meet this famous Brittney, but Mom wants to do a family day, you know, board games, and such…"

I laughed lightly. Ellie was an only child, so her family days were pretty quiet. She'd probably finish early and be able to come over anyway.

Still, I bid goodbye to her.

"Bye-o, Faye!" she said, and hung up.

The morning flew by. At 12:30, Mom went and looked out the window at the blizzard, which showed no signs of stopping. I scowled at the whiteness outside. It was March—shouldn't it be sunny and warm, rather than icy and cold?

"Brittney will probably still try to get here, even in this weather," Mom mused, coming back to the table and sipping her coffee—morning might have ended, but Mom's need for coffee hadn't. "Though I admire her determination, this is too dangerous. Your father didn't even go into work." It was true: my father had slept in, hung out with us for a bit, and now was in his office, the extra room attached to the master bedroom, sketching away yet again. "I have this new idea," had been his excuse, "and I have to draw it out before I forget."

Mom picked her phone up and scrolled through her contacts. "What was her number again?"

Mom was giving the Brittney the day off? This was a first. I inched closer, trying to listen in.

"Hello, Miss Fe—Brittney! How are you doing?.... I'm fine, thank you....Anyways, I'm sure you're aware of this snowstorm, and I just wanted to give you a call to let you know if you want the day off, it's yours. My husband didn't even go into work this morning, and I don't want you to have to risk these roads just for our clean house.... Haha, yes.... What?... You didn't need to, Brittney... Well... Okay. Brittney, you didn't need to, but okay, I appreciate it.... See you soon, then, I won't keep you distracted any longer. Thank you." She hung up and placed the phone on the table.

"What is it?" I asked expectantly.

"Apparently, she's already on the road here." I couldn't tell if Mom was happy or not with this ordeal. "She said it would be too late to turn back anyhow." Mom shook her head. "She's got real perseverance, is all I can say. I hope she stays safe on the roads."

"What does that mean?" Stella asked. She was coloring pictures in a coloring book at the kitchen table.

"What does *what* mean?" Mom said.

"That she's got 'real perseverance.' What's *perseverance?*"

"Determination, basically. It means nothing stops her from her work," Mom said.

"So she's still coming?" Stella asked, scrunching up her nose.

"Yes, she's still coming!" Mom said, exasperated.

"But didn't you say it's too dangerous for her to be out in the storm?" asked Stella, trying to figure it out.

"Stella Corcoran, I answered your question!" Mom snapped. "You don't need to keep asking more and more and more!"

"Sorry," Stella mumbled, sinking low in her chair. I looked from her to Mom, bewildered. Mom must be really tired, she was never that sharp with us.

Mom, catching me looking at her, sighed loudly, closed her eyes, then hoisted herself up from her chair and went into her bedroom, shutting the door behind her.

Stella looked at me with wide eyes. "That was weird," she said in a low voice.

I looked from her to Mom's closed door and nodded my agreement. "She's a lot more…tired than usual."

"And cranky," Stella added. "And tired. All the time."

"It could be why she hired Brittney," I said,

realization dawning. "Something's gotta be up, Stel. Something's amiss here. I know it."

"Know what?" Our conversation was interrupted as a snow-covered figure entered the house. His boots—as well as the rest of him—were caked in snow, and a half-frozen glove assisted him in shoving the back door shut. He started stamping his boots on the doormat, ridding himself of access snow, and then he began discarding his snowy gear until we could tell for certain was was our big brother.

"What were you doing out there, Jack?" Stella asked in a horrified voice.

"Frolicking in the snowy delight," Jack said sarcastically. Then, more seriously, he said, "Listen, can't a teenage boy go outside and have a good snowball fight with his friends without his lil' sisters worrying to death about him?"

"For your information," I said indignantly, "we weren't 'worrying to death.' Stella simply wanted to know. You'd do the same if we walked in covered in ice and snow."

"Guess you have a point." Leaving his frozen gear in a heap on the floor, he walked into the kitchen and stuck a cup of water in the microwave.

"What are you making?" Stella asked.

"Hot cocoa, silly."

"Can I have some?"

"Make it yourself." He dumped the contents of three cocoa packages in the cup and stirred vigorously. Ignoring the spots of chocolate that had sloshed onto the counter, he picked up the cup and took a gulp before ambling away.

"Wait!" Stella called, and he turned back, taking another gulp that left a chocolate mustache on his face. "Yeah, what do you want?"

"Come here." Stella looked around and beckoned.

Rolling his eyes, Jack took another drink and obliged, coming closer. "What, Stel?"

"Have you noticed any… unusual behavior from Mom?" Stella's voice was barely audible. I sighed, wondering how I didn't see this coming. Of course Stella was going to ask Jack his opinion.

"Are you kidding?" He took another long drink. "She's, like, overly cranky, overly tired, overly exhausted…Overly everything." Another gulp. I could tell he knew something.

"She's not herself at all anymore," Stella agreed.

"And if she's tired enough they hired Brittney"—I stopped, and looked at them—"then it's gotta be something serious."

Jack sighed. "If you'd listen to me…"

But Stella and me were on a roll, and everything strange we'd seen was coming out.

"She skips work all the time."

"She looks different."

"She refused a chocolate bar yesterday, and she *loves* chocolate."

"She sits on the couch all day."

"Guys!" Jack said, irritated. "I know what's

going on!"

We stopped, and looked at him.

"Here's the thing." He stopped a minute for suspense. "She acted the exact same way when she was pregnant with Stella. She was cranky and stuff, same as now, and then one day, don't you remember that, Faye? she told us, 'Guys, I'm pregnant.' "

We stared in disbelief at him.

"You're... I mean...you're saying..." I stammered.

Jack crossed his arms and leaned back, proud of himself. "Exactly!" he said. "I think she's pregnant!"

At first, Stella and I just stared. "Where's your proof?" I demanded, and Jack actually broke out laughing. "Proof? You want proof? Everything you just *said* is proof!"

"But how do we know your memory is accurate?" I cried. "I mean, *I* don't even remember that!"

"Well, you were really young," Jack responded dismissively. "Like, younger than Stella."

"Well, you were young then, too," I shot back.

"Yeah, but older than you," he said. "I'd be able to remember further."

Stella groaned, watching us argue. "Guys! It doesn't matter! What really matters is what Jack told us—Mom's pregnant!"

"Shh!" I snapped at her.

"Why the 'shhh'?" Jack asked me.

"Well, she obviously doesn't want us to know yet," I said. "She would have told us."

"Good point," he said. A grin spread over his face. "It'll be our secret." As he said so, he narrowed his eyes on me. "The Corcoran kids' secret. Which means no Ellie."

I laughed nervously. "I know, Jack. I won't tell her until Mom tells us officially."

"No," said Jack, his eyes still narrowed. "That means you don't tell Ellie at all. Until it's born."

I stared at him. "You got to be kidding!"

"Uh, duh!" he said grumpily. "Can't you recognize a joke when you see it?" Quickly he added, "You still can't tell her till we know for sure."

"I know," I repeated.

At that moment, we heard shuffling and then the master bedroom door creaked and Mom came out. Jack looked at us and said, "Conversation over!" as he dashed up the stairs, still holding his hot cocoa. Stella and I exchanged frantic looks and then rushed separate ways, her to the computer at the edge of the family room and me to the counter stools, where I pretended to be eating a cookie.

"You guys are sure in a hurry." A couple months ago, Mom would have noticed our secrecy immediately and called a family meeting on the spot to ask what was wrong. Now, she barely noticed a thing.

Further proving Jack's point.

She *had* to be pregnant! She just *had* to be!

Mom stood directly in front of me, looking in the fridge and trying to decide what to make for lunch. For a split second, I was tempted to just ask, *"Mom, are you pregnant?"* But I bit my lip, overcoming the temptation, remembering my promise to Jack and Stella that this was our secret until Mom told us. Besides, we probably weren't even supposed to know.

I kept my mouth shut as I slid out of the chair and exited the kitchen.

•　　•　　•　　•

Despite the snowstorm, Brittney arrived right on time, at one p.m. Of course. I watched her from the window as she walked up the snowy path, her hair tied in a tight bun, her scraggly coat pulled tight around her. Before she had a chance to knock, Stella and I had the door open. Brittney stepped inside gratefully. "Thanks, girls!"

"You're welcome," I said. "Was it hard to get here? How bad is the storm?"

"Pretty bad," Brittney said, shivering still as she hung up her coat. "The roads were okay, though. I might have trouble getting home."

I realized I had no idea where "home" was for Brittney. "Where do you live, Brittney?"

"Across town," she said, which didn't really explain anything, but I didn't press. I watched as she discarded the rest of her winter gear: put her boots by the door neatly, stuffed her mittens in her pocket. Her hat stayed, though, which I couldn't blame her. Even inside, the result of opening the door was a temporary chilly atmosphere in the foyer.

Stella and I followed her into the kitchen. Mom greeted her, thanking her again for coming out even in the storm. Brittney shook it off. "It's fine."

I found myself studying Mom carefully. She didn't look pregnant. Not yet, anyway. My heart fluttered at the thought that maybe she could be. I had never really given the topic much thought before. As long as I could remember, the Corcoran family comprised of my parents, Jack, me, and Stella. I had never imagined adding another member before. Now that I was imagining it, I found the idea quite appealing. Mom caught my spaced-out gaze, and I looked away, embarrassed.

Now there were two mysterious things in my house: our new house cleaner, and now the possibility of my mother being pregnant.

I wasn't getting anywhere with the pregnancy assumption. I followed Brittney as she went upstairs to clean the windows. "Who do you live with, Brittney?" I asked her absentmindedly.

"My friend," she replied. "In an apartment."

"Oh," I said, and after a moment, added, "Not with your siblings? Or parents?"

She seemed to stiffen. "No."

"Do you have any siblings?" I tried, knowing that I'd already asked her but feeling a bit bold.

She hesitated. Again, she gave me the same response in the same vague tone: "No."

I wanted to figure out why she seemed so vague, so hesitant, so protective around that subject, but she obviously didn't want to talk about it. Instead, I asked, "How long have you lived here? Like, in Forest Grove?"

"A few months," she said.

"Where did you live before?"

"California," she answered.

California! *Extra mysterious*, as Ellie would say. "That's far from here," I said. "Why'd you move here?"

"College," she said.

"You're not in college now," I pointed out.

"Faye, stop pestering the poor woman," Mom yelled at me from the family room below. She heard every word of my interrogation.

"It's fine, Mrs. Corcoran." Brittney smiled at me. "I don't mind questions." Then she said, "I'm taking some night classes right now, but mostly just working so next semester I can go full time."

"Oh," I said. Even if Brittney was on my side, I didn't want to get in more trouble with Mom. I didn't even know what was particularly wrong about it; Brittney was in my house all the time, and before now all I'd known about her was her first name and last name. I'd wanted to know more about her. Now that I thought about it, though, I didn't even remember her last name.

"What's your last name again, Brittney?" I asked.

"Ferry," she responded.

"Ferry like…?"

"The boat."

"Oh. Do—"

"Faye, stop bothering her," Mom shouted, clearly irritated.

Brittney didn't object, which told me maybe she did mind too many questions. I didn't ask any more.

•   •   •   •

"How's the Brittster doing?" Ellie asked me the following day at school. Unfortunately for us, we only had one day off for the snowstorm, and now it was back to the regular schedule. Luckily, though, it meant I could see my friends again.

"Who's the 'Brittster'?" Logan asked with raised eyebrows, munching on potato chips.

"Our cleaning lady," I said. "Her name's Brittney, but *somebody* likes to nickname people."

"What can I say?" Ellie cried. "It's who I am—the same way I call you 'Fayster' and Logan 'Logester', I *have* to call her Brittster. By the way, Faye, I have yet to meet this famous personnel."

"I have never once, in all my years of knowing

you, ever heard you call me 'Logester' or Faye 'Fayster'," Logan said, his face expressionless.

"Whatever, Logester," said Ellie without a moment's pause.

"Whatever, Ellster," retorted Logan immediately.

There was something about our whole situation, the whole conversation that struck me as funny. Apparently Ellie and Logan felt the same, too. We all exchanged quick glances, and then we all burst out into obnoxious laughter.

The other kids at the table made funny faces at us, and one boy even was daring enough to say, "What's so funny?" prompting us to laugh harder.

We calmed down after a minute, and discovered a table of kids waiting for an explanation. I hiccupped a few times, trying to figure out how to explain.

I knew most of the kids at the table: Emma from my English class, then Collin and Nate were from Math, and one other girl, Emma's friend, who sat with them. I thought maybe her name was Audrey. There were two others from my science class, too, but I didn't know their names. Not accustomed to our weirdness, they were now giving us an assortment of strange faces.

"Sorry," Logan mumbled finally. "Um...Ellie was being strange, and we got carried away. So it's nobody's fault." He pointed a finger at Ellie the whole time.

Ellie scowled. "Oh, don't listen to the old

Logester. The thing is, it's just really, really funny, and if you were sitting with us, you wouldn't have been able to stop, either."

"We *are* sitting with you," said one of the kids at the end of the table, a kid with braces and a sports T-shirt. "And you don't hear us laughing."

"That's funny." Ellie suddenly laughed. "Get it?"

"Laughter's contagious, you know," Logan commented.

"Then why aren't we laughing?" Emma said, crossing her arms.

"I don't know," said Ellie. "Maybe you're immune to laughter."

Her response had several people raising their eyebrows.

"See? Maybe you are!" said Ellie. "Hmm. Guess I'll have to test my theory, then."

"And how?" Audrey asked.

"Jokes!" declared Ellie. "Why did Logan cross the road?"

"Oh boy," groaned Logan.

When nobody answered, Ellie delivered the punch line: "To get to the grocery store to see its logo. Get it? Logan's nickname is 'Logo'?"

"It is?" Logan asked, growing exasperated.

"Well, it is now, anyway," said Ellie. "Okay, maybe that wasn't as funny as I'd hoped. How about this one. Knock, knock."

No answer.

"Okay, be that way. Faye, knock-knock," Ellie

said, turning to me. Then she reconsidered. "Never mind, the joke's about you. Logo! Knock-knock!"

Logan groaned—good naturedly, but loudly—and responded the standard phrase: "Who's there?"

"Faye."

Oh, boy.

"Faye who?"

"Fayster!"

I groaned at Ellie's apparent sense of humor. When still, nobody laughed, Ellie attempted a few more jokes before finally giving up. "Tough crowd, huh?"

"Apparently, Ellie." I shook my head. "Apparently."

The kids looked at us for a few minutes, weird expressions on their faces, before returning, reluctantly, to their meal.

chapter five
a simple piece of evidence

Weeks later, I arrived home from school
and was going upstairs to start my homework when
Brittney called to me. "Hey, Faye?"

I stopped and looked up. "Yeah?" This was a
first for Brittney to reach out to me, asking me
something. It had always been the other way
around. Maybe she finally felt like she knew me well
enough. I felt honored for some reason. As I'd
come to know Brittney over the last few weeks, I
found I liked her. Ellie, who still hadn't met her
(and was semi-furious about it) thought her
mysterious and suspicious (why she thought it
suspicious, I'll never know). Myself, I found her an
interesting character. She was friendly, kind, and yet
very secretive. When I asked her things, she'd
respond with the bare minimum of an answer, like

"Yes," "No," that sort of thing. It seemed to me like she was hiding something, but I kept my theory hidden from Ellie and let her imagine Brittney's behavior in her own way.

"Could you do me a big favor?" Brittney asked. "I forgot my phone in the car. Do you think you could run and get it for me? It should be right on the passenger seat."

"Um…"

My first thought was to ask Mom, and I looked around for her. When I couldn't locate her, I ran it over in my mind before deciding that there was no harm in helping. "Sure…I guess," I said carefully. I placed my backpack on the loft floor and went back downstairs.

"The car's unlocked." Brittney flashed me a grateful smile. "Thanks a lot, Faye."

"No problem." I slipped on my coat; after that one brief blizzard, the snow had mostly ceased, and the only thing remaining was the muddy slush covering the driveway and sidewalks. The air was still chilly and cold, though, and I stuffed my hands deeper in my pockets as I walked up to her car. Though I didn't mind doing a favor for her, I wondered why she couldn't do it herself.

Faded blue, rusty, and old, it was obvious Brittney didn't have much money, or at least not enough to afford a decent car.

The passenger door creaked loudly as I eased it open. The passenger seat was stained and ripped in one place. I winced. On the seat was a bag. I sifted through its contents: old scraps of paper, makeup, and pencils, that sort of stuff, but there wasn't any phone. Thinking that maybe it had fallen out, I leaned down to check the floor. The carpet was dirty, and I carefully tried to keep my hands from touching it much. Still, there was no phone to be found.

I checked in the driver's seat, under the driver's seat, and even scanned the backseat. No phone.

I had given up and was about to go back inside when something caught my eye, and I turned back.

It was a photograph, lying between the two seats. The few rays of sunlight reflected off it, making it shiny. Curious, I leaned across the seat and picked it up.

A younger Brittney, maybe twelve or thirteen, sits with a little girl in her lap. The little girl, who looks to be four or five years old, has bouncy brown curls pulled into two ponytails. Her eyes, bright and blue, are full of happiness, and she smiles widely up at me with such cuteness and innocence I can't help but smile myself, just looking at her. Brittney is reading the girl a book, and it looks like they've been interrupted for a picture. Brittney is smiling warmly as she looks at the camera, her arms encircling the little girl on her lap. Despite the age difference, there's no questioning they're related, probably sisters. A thought suddenly hit me.

Brittney had told me more than once that she didn't have any siblings.

I stared at the picture for a little while, unable to tear my eyes away. The little girl looked so familiar for some reason. Maybe she was in Stella's class at school. No, wait, that couldn't be right. This picture had to have been taken years ago; the girl would be a lot older now. Besides, hadn't Brittney said she'd used to live in California? If she had any siblings, they'd probably still be there.

Hmm.

I placed the picture exactly where I'd found it, and left the car. I walked slowly up the steps, just thinking. Inside, Brittney looked at me expectantly. It took me a minute to realize she was expecting the phone.

"Sorry!" I stammered. "I—I couldn't find it."

"Oh," said Brittney, disappointed. She looked around, and then, "Well, guess I'll go see if I have any luck." She turned and started towards the door.

"I can go look again," I faltered, but not before the door slammed behind her.

Upstairs, I was reluctant to start my homework. Not only was I not in any mood to figure out my algebraic equations—seriously, I didn't care what x equaled—but I kept wondering about the picture. I found it curious, mostly because Brittney had said she had no siblings. As I thought, a horrible possibility entered my mind. What if her sister had...*died*?

The thought lingered in my mind, but then I

brushed it away. Brittney wasn't the most cheerful girl I'd ever met, but she wasn't depressed or anything. She definitely didn't *look* like someone who'd lost a sibling.

Ellie would have some crazy theory about this whole thing. I had the urge to call her and tell her all about it, but then I remembered her knack for drama. If I wanted to actually talk, I would have to wait until I saw her in person. She would be impossible over the phone. I smiled, thinking about how lucky I was to have such a great, funny best friend.

Looking down at my math worksheets, I realized that it was already 3:15 and I hadn't started anything. I sighed. Even if the picture happened to be important, I couldn't do anything about it now anyway. I did my best to push the thoughts from my mind.

•　　•　　•　　•

That Friday, Ellie's wish was finally granted: she got to meet Brittney.

"Can I come by?" she'd breathlessly begged me on the phone at 3:30. "I zipped through my homework so fast just so I could! I can't stand another *minute* of not having met Brittney Brianna Ferry!"

"Brittney Brianna?" I said dubiously. "Ellie—"

"Okay, so *what* if I made it up?" Ellie said angrily. "*I* think it sounds good together! Think about it—*Brittney Brianna*? Anyways, *all* detectives refer to their clients by their first, second, and middle names. No, wait; they just use a middle initial, so I'd have to say Brittney B. Ferry. Doesn't that sound funny, Faye? Like, Brittney-Be-Ferry?"

I just listened to her ramble on, not even hiding the smile on my face, until finally she landed at her point. "Sorry for the distraction. I'm just super pumped. I'll be over in five."

"Ellie," I said, "you picked the wrong time to spend twenty minutes talking nonsense. She leaves in like ten minutes."

Ellie gasped. "Be over in a sec, then!" A quick pause suggested she had hung up, but then she said, "It's okay with your mom, right?"

"What? Course it is."

"Okay. Great. See ya." She hung up for real, and I replaced the phone, smiling. "Mom, it's okay if Ellie comes by, right?"

•   •   •   •

Brittney was just wrapping up her work when Ellie arrived. Ellie was literally jumping up and down. Brittney looked at her excitement with raised eyebrows.

"Brittney, this is Ellie. Ellie, this is—" I was

cut off by Ellie, of course. "Brittney, right?" she said eagerly. "I've heard *all* about you. You clean for the king of Europe, right?"

Brittney laughed for the first time I'd heard her and said, "Not quite. And so *you* are Ellie!"

"No, I'm the Queen of Europe. I heard about you because you clean for my husband, the King."

At this point I was doubled over laughing. Brittney just said, "Actually, Ellie, Europe is a continent, not a country, so there's not one ruler over it." She maintained a smile, telling me she was simply playing along. But there was a bit of moisture in her eyes, too, which made me wonder if we reminded her of something—*like a sister?*

Ellie was now faking sadness. "Aw, that's too bad, ain't it, Faye?" When I didn't answer, she said, "Back me up here, Britt."

"Guess it is." She checked her watch. "Oh, now I'm late. Nice to meet you, Queen Ellie. Bye, Faye."

Right before she left, she turned and faced our direction, though her eyes remained on the floor. "Oh, and guys? Please don't call me 'Britt' again, okay?"

Before we had a chance to answer, she was gone. We heard the rumble of her car engine before it drove away.

"Well, *that* sure went well," Ellie groaned. "Do you think I went too far? She probably thinks I'm some insane girl who actually thinks there's one ruler over Europe."

"I think it was hilarious," I said. "I mean, you got her to laugh, so that's good."

Serious Ellie was back. "Wait, do you mean she *doesn't* laugh normally?"

I groaned. "Cut it out...*Elisabeth M. Anderson*!" But I was laughing, even when she elbowed me in the stomach.

Ten minutes later, we headed up to my room, Ellie still muttering about "Brittney B. Ferry."

chapter six

a mystery invented by ellie

Despite the fact she had just been here, Ellie showed up at our house again the next day, except this time, it was planned beforehand that she would come home from school with me. Even though we did it frequently, the feeling of running home together from the bus stop, rather than our separate ways, was wonderful. Laughing, we ran down the street, hardly noticing the cold air. When we reached my empty driveway, Ellie stopped in disappointment. "What? Britt's not here today?"

"It's Thursday, Ell," I reminded her. "She's only here Mondays, Wednesdays, and Fridays."

"Ah, come on," said Ellie, disappointed. "Any other details you missed about…Brittney B—"

"Don't say it!" I laughed, and then, for some reason, the photograph I had seen in Brittney's car came to mind.

"Actually," I said, "there was one—I mean, I found one—uh—mysterious thing."

"There ya go, Fayster!" said Ellie, high-fiving me. "Got your detective hat on today, huh?"

"It wasn't today," I said. "It was a few days ago." Careful not to exaggerate, I told her what I'd found.

Ellie was wide-eyed, just as I'd expected. "Are you kidding me? Why, why, *why* did you not tell me before?"

I shrugged.

"This is *amazing*," Ellie breathed. "A real live *mystery*! Right in your own *home*!"

I groaned as I unlocked the door and let us in. Ellie got all the wrong impressions sometimes. "It's not a mystery, Ellie. It's just something...curious."

"Which is a mystery!" Ellie said. "I mean, seriously! Think of all the questions you have!"

One, I thought. *What about this is so exciting?* I mean, I thought it was interesting and all, but I didn't get Ellie's over-the-top enthusiasm.

"I know *I* have millions, and I haven't even *seen* the picture!" cried Ellie, and started exploding with questions and ticking them off on her fingers as we headed upstairs to my bedroom. "Who is the girl? Are they sisters? Good friends? Maybe she babysits her? How long ago was it taken? Where was it taken? How old is Brittney there? How old is the girl there? Who is the girl? Is the girl who looks like Brittney really Brittney?"

"*Ellie!*" I cried. "Stop! Is it really this big of a deal?"

"YES!" Ellie yelled at me. "This is *extraordinary*, Faye. It is *totally* this big of a deal. What if it's a tragic story Brittney needs help coping with?"

I stared at her. "*Coping* with? First of all, how do you even know there's anything to help with? And besides, she's like, seven years older than us. If anything, her own friends would help her. But us, for goodness' sakes? She barely knows who you are!"

"I know, I know," grumbled Ellie. "But at least accept it's a mystery. 'Cause it is."

I rolled my eyes.

"I saw that, Faye. You don't think this is a serious matter," Ellie challenged.

"Sure I don't," I said. "I mean, it's cool and curious and I'd love to know the story behind it. But do we really need to—"

"See! Ha! You admitted it," said Ellie. "You think it's a mystery."

"I said I think it's curious."

"That is a mystery, Faye."

I sighed. "What I mean is, I'm pretty sure that's Brittney and her sister. And if it is, then my questions are answered, for the most part, anyway. What else is there to ask, to discover, to do?"

"There's plenty," said Ellie. "All those questions I asked earlier! Who's going to answer them? Your mom? You?"

She was being sarcastic now, and we both knew it.

"Calm down, Ell," I said. "Either way, it's Brittney's personal life. We can't just intrude into her business. How about we talk about something else? Um...school? Logan wanting to dye his hair?"

"You're changing the subject on me," accused Ellie sourly, crossing her arms.

I sighed. Ellie was full of determination. "Well, what could we do now, anyway?"

"Brittney's here, right? We could talk to her."

"Look around, Ellie. Is she here?"

We were in my bedroom. Ellie went onto the loft and looked around. "She's disappeared."

"She was never here," I corrected.

"Come on," she said.

•　　•　　•　　•

Ellie seemed to be rubbing off on me more than ever since I'd told her about the photo I'd seen in Brittney's car. I found myself wondering about it to an extent that I hadn't before. The questions Ellie had asked kept returning to me, making me more curious. I feared sharing with Ellie would result in unnecessary drama, so I was alone in my thoughts.

Until one day, when there was a tentative knock on my bedroom door. I looked up, surprised. Who would knock? Was it Brittney? "Come in."

Stella hesitantly opened the door and stepped inside, shutting the door behind her. The look on her face was one of bewilderment and determination at the same time. Her curly hair was pulled into two uneven pigtails, suggesting she probably did it herself today. I watched her come over, push her bangs back, and sit on my bed.

"What is it, Stel?" I asked, leaning back in my desk chair.

Never one to think about what she'd say, Stella answered right away. "You and Ellie have a secret, and you're excluding me."

"What?" I said, flabbergasted.

"You like…I don't know. But you do. Don't you?" demanded Stella.

I looked at her.

"You guys talk all the time," she tried.

I laughed. "And we don't otherwise?"

"No, but…" Stella frowned, trying to find the words. "You're quiet about it. You go upstairs and shut the door."

"Yeah, once," I said.

Stella scowled at me and continued. "And then I hear Ellie sounding excited. But I can't tell what she's saying. And then you come out and never say anything. I told Mom and she says it's because you and Ellie have a secret."

"You told Mom?"

"Yeah, but I don't think she really meant the whole secret thing," Stella confided. "She only said it so I'd stop asking her questions."

"Really?" Mom wasn't usually that short with Stella. Another piece of evidence towards our pregnancy theory. A thrill shot through me—*it had to be true.*

"Just tell me your secret," Stella said sourly.

What did she even mean by secret? We'd only closed the door and acted secretive about the picture, and that'd only been once, or maybe twice at the most. Still, I knew that just once would be enough for Stella.

Our "secret" had to be the picture.

"I'm sorry, Stella," I started, just to clarify we were on good terms with one another. "I guess it has been sort of a secret, though we didn't mean to make it one."

Stella fidgeted in anticipation. "What *is* it?"

"I found a picture," I said. "In Brittney's car."

Stella was scarcely breathing, taking in my every word with an intrigued look on her face. I willed myself to not get annoyed. She was worse than Ellie. Except with Ellie's drama, I smiled and shook my head. I thought, guiltily, of how different it was with Stella: instead of giggling, I got annoyed.

"There were two girls in the picture," I went on. "One was Brittney, when she was younger. And—"

"How did you know it's Brittney?" Stella interrupted, wide-eyed.

I sighed, trying to keep my annoyance hidden. "I could just tell, okay, Stel? Anyway, it was of Brittney and another little girl."

"Who?" breathed Stella.

I threw my hands up. "I don't know, Stella! Ellie and I think it's her sister, because it looks like her. But Brittney says she has no siblings."

"Oh!" Stella said. "What else did Ellie say?"

I snorted. "She thinks it's a huge mystery."

Stella frowned. "Oh. But don't you want to find out more about it?"

I shrugged. "To a certain extent."

"What does that even mean?" cried Stella.

"It means if we don't go overboard with it." I sighed and looked back at my notebook, where I'd been working on a history report before Stella interrupted me.

"Oh. Okay." Stella sat, cross-legged, on my bed as I bent over to finish the last few sentences. The pencil scratched across the paper, and Stella sat there and waited. After a few minutes, I said, "Why are you still here, Stel?"

She scowled. "Why are you so mean?"

"I'm not," I said. "I'm just wondering."

"Oh." Stella shrugged and flopped back on my pillows. "I don't know. Just thinking, I guess."

I wanted to be alone, to think by myself privately, but I didn't know how to ask her to leave. Deciding she was probably in the same situation, I let her hang around. I finished my report, and then we both just sat there, me in my chair and her on the bed, thinking.

chapter seven
sibling meeting

"Jack?" I knocked timidly at his door—just like the way Stella had knocked on mine the previous day—and then pushed it open. Mom wasn't home and Dad was at work, so this was the best time to discuss with Jack about our theory. We had another piece of evidence.

When I arrived home from school, Mom was dressed nicely and putting makeup on. I looked at her. "What are you doing?"

"Don't be disrespectful, Faye," she chastised.

I still looked at her. "Where are you going, though?"

"Just some errands." I knew instantly that wasn't true; why look for errands? "No, Mom, where are you *really* going?" I pressed.

She glared at me. "I told you. I have an errand

to run really quick. I'll be back by five, maybe five-thirty."

It was only three now. "A two and a half hour errand?"

She sighed. "Stop the questions, Faye. Go start your homework."

I shrugged. "Okay. Bye, then."

She kissed me on the cheek. "Bye, honey."

Upstairs, I'd carefully worked until I heard the garage door creak shut. Then I had tiptoed over to Jack's room.

Now, he grumbled, "What's it?"

"Can I come in?" I asked, peeking inside.

There was a pause. "Yeah, fine."

I stepped into the dark room. Though his window was wide, he shaded the sunlight with thick, dark shades. The room was painted a navy blue, creating, overall, a dark, dense atmosphere. Here and there were surprisingly bright glow-in-the-dark items.

Jack sat at his desk, working by the light of his lamp, and spun around when I came in. "What's it?" he said again.

I hesitated, and looked around to ensure our privacy even though I knew the only other person in the house, Stella, would hear this eventually anyway. "Do you know where Mom went?"

"No, she just said she was going someplace. Why does it matter?" he asked with disinterest.

I told him about my conversation with Mom, how she had been reluctant to tell me exactly where she was going.

Jack leaned back in his chair, thinking it over. "Suspicious. What, exactly, does it mean, though?"

I stared, surprised he hadn't caught on. "If she's pregnant like you think she is—"

"Oh, she *totally* is," Jack agreed enthusiastically.

I glared at him. "—if she is, then eventually she'll have a doctor's appointment." Now it was Jack staring at me, starting to grasp it. "So you're saying that's where she went today?"

"She got, like, dressed up," I said. "And why else would she refuse to tell us?"

Jack stood up and paced the room. "She can't keep it a secret forever." Suddenly he stopped and spun around. "Where's Stel?"

"You want Stella to be a part of this?" This was new, Jack going out of his way to include his sisters.

"Oh, it's just going to be me and you, and we'll totally leave her the only one out?" he said sarcastically. "It'll be a pain if we don't. I mean, she already knows Mom's pregnant. Go get her, will you?"

I rolled my eyes, but obliged. Stella, sprawled across her bed, looked up from her book indignantly when I pushed her door open and told her to come to Jack's room for a sibling meeting. "You always pick on me, just because I'm the youngest!" she accused sourly, crossing her arms.

I sighed. "No, Stel, this is serious. Come on." I

turned and left, waiting for her to follow, and sure enough, I heard a loud groan and then her footsteps behind mine.

In Jack's room, Jack shared our theory with Stella. Even though she had already known about the pregnancy idea, the whole new piece of evidence shocked her. "Really?" she breathed.

"*Really*," Jack said, mimicking her tone. I glared at him, and he reluctantly dropped the act. For once, Stella hadn't even noticed. "This is real?"

"No, it's totally fake," Jack said.

I ignored him. "Why else would we tell you, Stel?"

Stella's eyes darted from me to Jack, and then slowly, a grin began spreading across her face. "I'm going to be a big sister," she said, overjoyed.

"So am I," I told her.

"But you've been one before, when I was born." Stella was aghast. "I've never been a big sister, not once. This is amazing!" Then she lowered her voice. "Is Mom going to officially tell us, you think?"

"Well, she's got to eventually," I said, looking to Jack for guidance.

"Faye-Faye's right," he said. "Eventually she'll have a big stomach, and if she doesn't tell us, we'll all think she's just fat, and Mom doesn't want people to think she's fat. Of course," he added quickly, "if that did happen, *we* would know what was up."

I shook my head at my brother's craziness. "I

guess Jack has a point. She does have to tell us eventually. And she'll have lots of doctor's appointments, too."

"Right," Jack caught on. "And if she doesn't tell us, then she'll be forced to lie to her own precious children over and over, at least whenever she has an appointment."

I bit my lip to keep my comments back. Stella had no such willpower. "You are crazy, Jackson!"

"Hey," he said warningly, "Don't let me catch you calling me that again."

Stella grinned. "Okay, Jackson."

"I mean it, Stel!" He actually sounded fierce this time. I gave Stella a warning glance.

"Fine," she grumbled. Then she perked back up. "So, what do we do now? Should we ask Mom?"

After a moment of indecision, Jack said, "No. Not yet. We wait for her to tell us. And fake utter shock when you do. We don't want her knowing how smart we are."

I rolled my eyes.

"What in the world?" Stella cried.

"I'm joking, okay?" he said.

I sighed. "Yep, you're always joking."

"Not always," he defended himself.

Stella groaned, loudly. "But what do we do, then, if we're not asking Mom?"

Jack shrugged, appearing disinterested. "Nothing, I guess. Wait. Watch."

Stella looked at him. "What?"

"You heard me," he replied. Then he looked at his sheets of homework, then at us. "Well, what are you standing around for? I got homework to do. Go away."

Irritated, I left the room. Stella followed behind, complaining loudly, but I ignored her complaints.

chapter eight
secrets revealed

Our watching and waiting concerning the pregnancy did not last long. Our suspicions were officially confirmed that night at dinner.

Mom had said she'd be home by dinnertime, but Dad arrived home and she still wasn't. He was startled when he looked around and she wasn't here. "Where's your mother?" he asked Jack.

Jack shrugged. "She wouldn't tell us where she went. But she *did* say she'd be home by now."

Dad grumbled something under his breath and took out his cell phone. "Hello? Kimberly?...You okay?...Yeah, where are—Oh, yeah!...Okay. See you soon, honey." He replaced the phone in his pocket.

Jack, Stella, and I stood eagerly, anxiously, waiting.

Dad laughed. Whatever Mom had told him certainly had lightened his mood. "You guys already know, don't you?"

Stella and I exchanged looks, but Jack was on top of it. "We certainly do. That was a doctor's appointment, wasn't it?"

Dad laughed again. "And do you know the rest?"

"You betcha," Jack said right as I was wondering what, exactly, the rest was. "Mom's pregnant. I'm a big boy, Dad. I remember what she was like when she was pregnant with Stel."

Dad grinned. "Surprise!" he said to us. "Jack's right. You're going to have a new baby brother or sister soon!"

We'd all already known it, but still, the kitchen was full of laughter and cheering, excitement and joy, that it was true, really true.

After the chaos calmed down, Jack raised his eyebrows in suspicion. "Wait a second. The appointment wasn't to tell whether boy or girl?"

Dad chuckled. "We decided not to find out. You know, a surprise?"

Jack and Stella stared at him, disbelieving. "*What?*" Stella cried. "I'll have to actually wait until the baby's born to know?"

"That's right," Dad said cheerfully. "What's wrong with it?"

"I don't know! I just don't like it," Stella whined, crossing her arms.

"Me neither," huffed Jack. "What if it's girl?

Not only will I be totally and unfairly outnumbered, but I'll have my hopes up about a boy and then those hopes will be destroyed!"

Dad sighed and turned to me. "What do you think, Faye?"

I considered my words carefully. "I think it'll be fun, not to know. And a big surprise when it's born."

"Well said, Faye," he said.

•　　•　　•　　•

Mom walked in from the garage entrance a little while later. She'd stopped at a drive-thru on the way home and picked up dinner for us, and we ate in the family room. Mom was happy, excited, thrilled; she apologized, later, for being short with me earlier.

"Your father and I weren't sure when we were going to tell you," she said. "But I shouldn't have been so rude. I'm sorry."

"It's okay." I was too happy to be mad. "I can't wait. What's the due date, exactly?"

"August twenty-fourth."

I grinned.

"Could be sooner, could be later," Dad said from across the room. "Babies sometimes come early. And sometimes come late."

"The doctor thinks it might come a little early," Mom said. She and Dad shared a knowing

glance. I wondered what it meant, and hoped it was simply another surprise, not something wrong.

●   ●   ●   ●

I held my tongue and suppressed the strong, nearly-overwhelming urge to tell Ellie on the bus. If I did, not only would she pry from me every detail, but she would tell Logan, and I wanted to tell him myself. The only option was to wait until lunch.

However, Ellie knew me too well to go with my act that nothing was up. "What's your secret, Fayster?" Ever since she made up that name a few weeks ago, it was pretty much all she called me. And Logan's new name was "Logo." She had, at first, insisted on "Logester," but Logan had persisted against it so vehemently that she had finally relented to "Logo." It didn't stop Logan from hating it, and he stuck his tongue out at her whenever she used it, but from what I understood, it wasn't as bad as "Logester."

Now, I looked at her and bit my lip. "I'll tell you at lunch."

"Ah, come on!" she exclaimed. "Are you seriously expecting me to wait until lunch to know this huge secret?"

"Well, Logan deserves to know any secret this big as well, right?" I said.

"You mean Logo?" she said, then added,

reluctantly, "Yeah, guess so. But why can't you tell me now, and him later?"

"Because you'll freak out and tell him before I can," I said.

Ellie looked guilty. "Listen, I can't help who I am, right?"

I laughed. "Just wait, okay? Just wait."

"*Wait* is *not* a word in my vocabulary," Ellie responded fervently.

"Well, now's a good time as any to add it in there." I crossed my arms. "My lips are zipped until lunch."

•   •   •   •

When lunchtime finally arrived Ellie sat in her seat and grabbed my arm. "I've suffered the whole morning, Faye. Spill the beans."

"Spill the beans about what?" Today Logan had shaped his hair into a mohawk, but his hair was too short to make a complete one so it mostly looked like his hair was drastically messed up.

"Faye has a secret and she won't tell me," Ellie said accusingly. "She put me through the torture of making me wait so she could tell you, too."

"Really?" Logan smoothed his hair back, but it popped right back into its strange mohawk shape immediately. "I'm flattered."

I scowled at him.

"Cut the dillydallying and tell us already, Fayster!" Ellie cried.

I scowled at Logan a minute longer to spite Ellie, then took a breath, smiled, and looked at them. I couldn't hold it in a minute longer. "My mom's pregnant!"

There was a moment of silence. Then Ellie squealed, "Pregnant? As in, you get a new sibling? AAAAAAAAAH!" she yelled. "You are the absolute luckiest girl *EVER*—"

"That's great, Faye," Logan interrupted. "D'ya know if it's a boy or girl?"

"No, they're gonna let it be a surprise." The thought sent a thrill through me. I could have a baby brother soon. Or a sister!

At that, Ellie, who'd been rambling on and on how lucky I was and what an amazing thing this was, suddenly stopped her chattering and gasped. "*Really*? That's awesome!"

"Um, thanks?"

"No, really, it's *incredible*. Imagine all the fun we'll have making guesses!" Ellie cried.

Logan leaned on his elbow, stuck a pretzel in his mouth, and looked at her with his eyebrows raised.

"Making guesses?" he repeated slowly. "And there are more than two to make?"

Ellie ignored him and looked at me. "Make sure I'm the first to know, you know, when it's born, 'kay?"

"I'm pretty sure my parents will know first,

Ell."

"Fine, then after that."

"How about me and Jack and Stel?" I said. "How can I tell you if I don't know myself?"

Ellie crossed her arms and then took a bite of her sandwich. "Fine. But after your family knows, I'm first."

"Fine," I replied, because I knew no other answer would satisfy her.

"Good." Ellie promptly bit into her sandwich.

While her mouth was full and therefore she was temporarily unable to contribute to the conversation, Logan leaned over and whispered in my ear, "We need a good nickname for Ellie. You know, to get back."

"Yes," I said out loud. "We do."

Ellie swallowed. "We do what?" she asked innocently.

"Nothing, *Ellster*," Logan said loudly. Ellie didn't react to the nickname. I leaned over to Logan and whispered, "Discuss this later."

In reply, he winked.

Ellie sighed loudly. "So, Faye, have you decided on any names for the baby?"

I laughed. "We just found out, like, yesterday, Ellie. I mean, my parents might be thinking of some. But we haven't as a family."

"How do you know you will discuss it as a family?" Ellie demanded. "When Jessica was born, my parents didn't tell me her name until I got to hold her for the first time."

"Jessica's your *cousin*, Ellie," I said. "That's not the same. Your parents probably didn't even know her name until then."

Ellie pouted. "But Faye, you have siblings. I don't. It's only fair. I get to know the name as soon as you do. First, middle, third, fourth, however many names you decide to give it. Okay?"

I sighed. "Fine, fine, fine."

"Good, good, good."

•   •   •   •

As I suspected, Ellie was crazy about the whole thing the rest of the day. Throughout classes, she'd always manage to catch my eye, making "wow" faces at me, and sometimes pantomiming a baby in her arms. I rolled my eyes and looked away.

Ellie was my best friend. But sometimes, too much drama is too much drama.

chapter nine
item from the past

As summer grew closer, Ellie began counting down the days until school let out. It was the one part of spring Logan and I joked we hated—Ellie's counting-down time. This year, she came up with a chant she pretty much said all day long — "Twenty-days until summer, summer, summer, summer, yeah! Twenty-days until summer, summer—"

"*ELLIE*!" Logan would shout. "We get the point! Twenty days until summer! You can cut the song!"—but he was never truly mad, and it never really helped anyway.

As the temperature continued to rise, the desire to go to school lowered and lowered, especially for Ellie. Sometimes, in the morning, I'd get calls from her: "Faye, the thermostat says it's seventy-five, there's barely a breeze, and the sun's out. How can I go to school and stay inside all day?"

I'd usually respond with, "How about we go outside when we get home?" That would usually persuade Ellie, though sometimes she would protest longer.

One particular day, I slept through my alarm and once I awoke, I scrambled to get ready on time. Shaking the last remnants of sleep from my eyes, I randomly chose an outfit and hurriedly dressed. I ran a comb through my hair and ran downstairs.

Mom small-talked cheerily on the phone downstairs. When she saw me, she smiled. "Oh, here's Faye now. Here she is." She handed me the phone while mouthing, "Ellie."

Of course, Ellie. Who else could it be?

I took the phone and pressed it to my ear. "What's up, Ell?"

"Faye, the sun's shining. Want to head to the bus stop now and enjoy the glorious summertime sunshine before the bus arrives?"

"That whole statement just rhymed," I said. "And sure, I guess." My stomach rumbled then, reminding me I still hadn't had breakfast. At the same time it also occurred to me my bag wasn't ready.

"I'll need a few minutes to eat and stuff," I told Ellie sheepishly. She sighed loudly over the phone. "Hurry, then. I'll be out there, 'kay?" She hung up.

" 'Kay," I echoed, even though I knew she

couldn't hear me.

•   •   •   •

I scarfed down a bowl of cereal, stuffed my things in my bag, pulled my hair into a side ponytail. I could braid it once I got to the bus stop. I said goodbye to Mom and Stella, and rushed out the door.

The morning air was crisp and cool. The sun shined, and I welcomed the rays of warmth. I looked up to see Ellie at the stop at the end of the street; when she saw me, she waved excitedly.

I waved back and started down the driveway, but stopped halfway as something caught my eye. The sunlight reflected off its shiny surface, and it laid there, standing out amongst the remaining slushy snow. I bent down, picked it up, and froze.

It was a photograph—one I'd seen before.

Brittney's face stared up at me, along with the face of the sweet-looking little girl.

The same picture I'd seen in Brittney's car had somehow ended up in my driveway and was now in my hands.

Holding it, I stared in disbelief. There was something off about the picture, but I couldn't put my finger on it. Instead, I found myself studying it, noticing the little details I hadn't before. The little blue and pink striped dress. Brittney's pink jacket.

The little girl's cute pigtails.

I figured Brittney had probably dropped it, accidentally, the previous day, and I looked around, unsure of what to do. Finally I resolved to slip the photograph in my pocket and resumed walking to the bus stop.

•   •   •   •

Ellie was waiting expectantly. "Well?"

"Well, what?"

"What'd you find?"

I wasn't sure if I wanted to tell her yet. "Huh?"

"You found something on your driveway," she said slowly. "I *saw* you."

"Oh," I said. "It was nothing."

"Faye, you put it in your pocket."

"It was just...chalk."

"Chalk? You're my best friend, Faye, I know when you're lying."

"I'll tell you later," I promised.

She crossed her arms. I didn't say anything. The bus pulled up, and we boarded. I slid into the seat next to the window, and sat, thinking, fingering the picture in my pocket.

•   •   •   •

I was awkwardly aware of the folded picture in my pocket the whole day, and I kept patting my pocket to reassure myself it was there and hadn't fallen out. What if I lost it? It wasn't even mine; it was Brittney's. I was afraid to put it in my bag for fear someone would find it; my pocket was the only place I felt I could keep an eye on it, somewhat.

Ellie kept a strange look on me all morning, but didn't say anything. She knew, as well as I, that I couldn't keep a secret for long.

Logan was mysteriously absent that day. He was probably just sick, but with Ellie, any absence was mysterious. So at lunchtime, it was just me and Ell at the end of the table. Ellie thumped her lunch bag down, reached over, and grabbed my arm. "Spill the beans, Faye, you can trust me, and besides, I'm your BFF forever."

I took a breath. "Fine. Okay. Remember the picture I told you about?"

She looked at me blankly.

"The one from Brittney's car?" I prompted.

"Oh! That one?" Ellie said, aghast. "You really thought I'd forget? Of *course* I remember!"

Lacking any other words, I reached into my pocket, retrieved the picture, and set it on the table. "Well, here it is."

Ellie's jaw dropped.

"How long have you had this?" she demanded, grabbing it and holding it up to the light to get a better look.

"Ellie, I found it on my driveway this

morning."

"Aha! That's what it was." Ellie was awed. "This is it, though? I mean, *it*?"

"Um, guess so," I said.

"Wow." Ellie studied it intensely, just like I had known she would. "That's definitely Brittney. And the girl—there's an obvious resemblance there. They look like sisters."

"That's what I thought," I said. I took out an apple and bit into it as I leaned over to get a look. Ellie had temporarily abandoned her lunch, which still sat in her bag, to instead look at the picture. I had no intention of starving just to look at a photograph.

"Did I hear a catch in your voice?" said Ellie suspiciously. "What do you know that I don't?"

"Remember, Brittney says she has no siblings?"

"Oh! Duh! Why is she lying?" Ellie jabbed a finger at the picture. "That's her sis! Anyone who tells me otherwise is crazy."

I took another bite of my apple, watching Ellie, who returned to studying it. "It could *not* be her sister, you know, Ellie."

"What?"

"I mean, Brittney doesn't have a reason to lie to me. Maybe it's just her neighbor."

Ellie looked at me.

"Cousin, maybe?"

Ellie cocked her head, contemplating my words. "You have a point there, Fayster. I mean,

Brittney's a pretty honorable, trustworthy cleaning lady."

I rolled my eyes.

"You're right. It could be her cousin. Or maybe it's a, like, long lost sister she doesn't know is her sister and she thinks is her cousin."

I lifted my eyebrows. "What?"

"Anything's possible, Faye! You're not thinking outside the box." Ellie held the picture close to her face. "I mean, it could be anybody! It could be *me*! Look at her curls. Pretty close to mine, don't ya think?"

"Or it could be her neighbor," I said.

"Or it could be *you*!" Ellie said excitedly.

"Maybe her cousin," I said.

"Or my *mom*!"

"Her niece?"

"Or *Stella*!"

"Maybe it's her second-cousin, then."

"Or that girl over there at that table! See, the one with the blue headband? She has curls *just* like these."

"Maybe it's just a girl she babysits."

"Or *Logan*!" Ellie breathed.

At that, I just looked at her. "Logan's a boy, Ellie," I said.

"Yeah, I know, so what?"

"That—" I indicated the picture —"is a girl."

"Oh." Ellie shrugged. "Just throwing the ideas out there!"

After a while she said, "Can I come to your

house today after school?"

"I can ask my mom." I was used to Ellie inviting herself over.

"What's today?"

"May fourteenth."

"No, what day of the week? Sunday, Monday, Tuesday?"

"Wednesday?" I said.

"Perfect! The Brittster's at your house, then?"

"Um, yes?" I said, afraid of where this was going.

"It's settled, then," said Ellie, and reached over for a high-five I refused to give her. Shrugging, she suddenly noticed her lunch and reached into her bag, pulling out an orange. Peeling it, she turned back to me and opened her mouth, then noticed what I was eating and sidetracked. "Hey, we both have fruit!"

I sighed. "What were you going to say, Ell?"

"Oh! Yeah. Well, we're *obviously* talking to Brittney about this."

"What?" I cried, knowing all the possibilities "talk" could mean in Ellie's vocabulary.

"Why not? It's a *perfect* opportunity."

"Ellie, my mom will never let us walk up to Brittney and ask her about her personal, private life," I said, deadpan.

"Why not?"

"Ellie, did you not catch the words 'personal' and 'private'?"

Ellie sighed. "Faye, a piece of her 'personal

and private' " —Ellie made air quotes—"life fell on your driveway. How else can we return it to her?"

She had a point. I looked at the photograph, which was laying on the table, for a few minutes as I finished up my apple. Ellie leaned over and stole some pretzels from my lunch. "Your food's getting cold, Faye."

I rolled my eyes. "Like it was ever warm to begin with?"

Ellie ignored me. "So, I'm coming over after school, right?"

I sighed. "I'll ask my mom."

•　　•　　•　　•

Ellie persisted on staying at the bus stop while I ran to my house to ask if Ellie could come.

"Ellie, you might not be able to come," I said. "You could just go home and I can call you. Besides, doesn't your mom need to know?"

Ellie shrugged. "I can just call her from your house."

I sighed and turned, going back towards my house; Ellie's house was in the opposite direction of the stop.

When I walked inside, Mom smiled at me from the couch. "Hello, sweetie. How was school?"

"Fine. Can Ellie come over?"

"Now?" she said.

I nodded eagerly.

Mom sighed. "Okay, but only until five, okay?"

"Aw, can't she stay for dinner?"

Mom sighed again. "Not tonight, Faye. Five o'clock or nothing."

"Fine," I grumbled, and turned to go tell Ellie, and then stopped. "Where's Brittney?"

"Kitchen." Mom looked at me sternly. "Make sure you and Ellie stay out of her way. I know Ellie, and I don't want her pestering Brittney."

I swallowed, thinking of the picture in my pocket and Ellie's outrageous plans. "I'll tell her not to," I said, then went outside and gave her thumbs-up.

Ellie ran at my signal, her wild red hair flying behind her and her backpack jostling back and forth. When she got to my house she was panting, and stopped for a minute to catch her breath. Her eyes fell on Brittney's car in the driveway. "Man, is that one old car."

"You can say that again," I agreed. "I wonder how it even drives."

"Another question onto the 'Brittney List'!" Ellie said cheerily.

I sighed. "My mom doesn't want us bothering Brittney," I said.

"Oh, we won't," Ellie assured me.

I led the way inside, not sure whether to believe her or not.

As I came inside, Stella, who had apparently

gotten a half-day at school, came rushing down the stairs excitedly. "Who's there?"

"Only Ellie, Stella," I said.

"Aw, come on," said Stella, crossing her arms and turning to go back upstairs.

I laughed. "What, were you expecting someone?"

"No, I just wish someone would come to see me once. You always have friends over. And I never do."

"Never what?" Ellie asked, coming in after me (she had once again become sidetracked over something of interest on my porch). She rushed to hug Stella in greeting, who was coming downstairs reluctantly. I rolled my eyes good-naturedly at Ellie's never-stopping over-the-top kindness to my somewhat annoying, somewhat sweet little sister.

"Stella was expecting someone, I think," I laughed. "And you do too have friends over, Stel. Take last week, for example. What was her name, the girl who came home with you on the bus?"

Stella scrunched up her nose. "Who?"

I sighed. "You guys hid in your room and played dolls the whole time?"

"Oh, Kaitlyn. Yeah, she came over. But that only once, Faye. Ellie's here like every single day."

"But I live on the same street," Ellie said. "All I have to do is take a brisk, quick, five-minute-walk, and wha-la! Here I am. And anyways, I am *not* here 'every single day.' If that was the case, I'd be sick of Faye by now."

I elbowed her. "And Stella," I added, "how about those neighbor girls across the street? They seem to be outside with you a lot during the summer."

"They don't live across the street," Stella said spitefully. "They live *down* the street. Like five houses. And that's during summer. I'm talking about *now*."

"Summer's approaching faster than you think," Ellie commented.

"She's right," I said. "How many more weeks of school, Ellie?"

"You mean *days*," Ellie corrected me. "How many more days of school. Fifteen! Fifteen, fifteen, fifteen!" Then suddenly, she lowered her voice and looked around. "Where's the Brittster?"

"Cleaning out the oven," Stella answered promptly.

"What?" squealed Ellie.

"She's cleaning the oven out," Stella repeated, and I hurried to say, "Her job includes more than just dusting and vacuuming, you know. Somebody's gotta do the hard work, and you know my mom isn't up to it."

"Why?"

"Uh, have you forgotten she's pregnant?"

"Ooooh! Yeah! That's amazing!" Ellie cried. Then she looked around sheepishly, and said, quieter, "Okay, I get it. Let's go find her."

"Where are you going?" Stella demanded from the stairs.

"Ssssh!" Ellie said. "Come on, Stel. We've got a serious mission."

"Aw, Ellie, isn't this just our mission?" Then I realized what she'd said. "Wait, Ellie, a *mission?*"

"Uh, yeah, a mission! And why can't Stel be apart? She's got some good ideas, you gotta admit, Faye." Ellie, without waiting for my consent, dragged a beaming Stella into our circle. Including Stella wouldn't have been my first choice, but she looked so thrilled that there wasn't any way I could kick her out now.

"Fine. But let me and Ellie do the talking," I told her. She nodded wordlessly, her green eyes wide.

"Where's the picture, Faye?" asked Ellie.

I pulled it out of my pocket, unfolded it, and handed it to her.

"Intriguing," Ellie whispered. "Look at them. Carefully. We've got to commit this page to memory before we hand it over."

"Why?" Stella breathed, enthralled.

"Because it's important to study all works of evidence," Ellie replied. She continued. "Note the simple, but elegant, stripes across the little girl's dress—stripes in deep tones of magenta, aqua, and brown. Note the way her hair is parted in two pigtails. Note Brittney's lovely pink sweater. Note Brittney's nice—"

"We get the point, Ellie," I laughed.

"But this is the evidence! For our case!" she cried. "We need to have every inch memorized!"

Before I could remind her this wasn't a case, this wasn't evidence, she had folded the picture back up and returned it to my hand, muttering something about how nobody appreciated the work of detectives. Then she froze. "Wait. You didn't fold this ancient work of art, did you, Faye?"

"What?"

"The picture," she hissed. "Was it already folded when you found it?"

"I don't know," I said. "I don't remember."

"Faye, Faye, Faye," she said, shaking her head in mock disapproval. Then she resumed her important voice. "This is the battle plan. Faye will—"

"Battle plan?" I repeated.

"Go along with it, Fayster. I'll introduce us. Faye will present the photo. I'll back you up. And Stella, just stand there and look innocent. Alright?"

Stella nodded eagerly. "Let's go!"

Ellie led the way into the kitchen. She insisted we sneak around corners, slide behind couches, and otherwise act like spies. I rolled my eyes but followed along. Stella, of course, loved it. Finally Ellie reached the kitchen, waited until Brittney's back was turned, and motioned for us all to stand up. We did.

"Ahem. Brittney?"

Brittney stood up, placed a bundle of blackened rags on the countertop, wiped her brow, and turned to us wearily. "Hey, girls." She retrieved a fresh rag and bent down to finish up the job.

I didn't even have to look at Ellie to know what she was thinking: *this won't work*. How could we present a photo if she's not standing up to see it?

Ellie cleared her throat. "Um, Brittney? We found something...mysterious."

Yep, that was Ellie, making something mostly normal seem mysterious. I hid a grin—and an eye roll—and stealthily passed Ellie the picture behind my back, knowing she was going to want it.

"Mysterious, huh?" Brittney said without looking up, only shoving her sleeves up higher.

"I—that is, we—think it belongs to you."

At that, Brittney turned to look at us, confused. "What?"

Ellie took a moment for drama, dragging out the moment for as long as possible. "Faye found this on her driveway. Is it yours?"

As she finished speaking, Ellie moved the picture from behind her back and held it facedown to Brittney.

Brittney gasped. She wiped her hands off on a towel and rushed forward, taking it from Ellie's hands. She flipped it over and gasped again. "Oh!" she said, wordless.

"It's yours, then?" Ellie said calmly.

I suddenly remembered that Mom had told us not to bother her, and guilt swept over me, despite the fact I really hadn't had much choice in the matter. I realized we would have had to give the picture to Brittney at some point either way, and reassured myself by telling myself that it'd be fine—

as long as Ellie didn't go any farther.

"Yes," Brittney said, and blinked a few times; her eyes almost looked teary. "Yes, it's mine. I've been missing it. Where did you say you found it?"

"My driveway. I found it this morning, on my way to school," I said.

"Probably dropped it, then," said Brittney softly, mostly to herself. Then she looked up. "This is very important to me. How can I thank you enough?"

"It's fi—" I started to say, but of course, Ellie had other ideas.

"It's no problem, Brittney," she said, "but may we ask one question?"

Oh no...here we go.

Brittney walked around the counter island to carefully zip the picture into her small shoulder bag. "Yeah, I guess."

"Who's the girl?"

Brittney turned, alarmed, and so did I.

"Ellie—!" I cried.

Ellie ignored me and looked at Brittney, expectantly.

Brittney stopped to think, and ran a hand across her forehead. "Me."

"No, the little girl."

"The..." Brittney trailed off, and suddenly her gaze was fixated on me sharply. I felt uncomfortable, and when I looked up again, her eyes were distant, vague. "That'd be...my sister."

Sister?

Brittney remained vague as she continued. "My sister died," she said flatly. "She was in a car wreck when she was five."

I blinked twice and stared at her, trying to comprehend what I'd heard. Brittney had a sister? Who died in a car accident? At age *five*? *That had to be why the picture was so important!* Emotions surged through me and sympathy emerged towards Brittney.

Always the drama queen, Ellie's eyes instantly clouded. "Brittney, that's awful!"

I had never even known Brittney's sister. I felt tears brimming in my own eyes. I blinked them away.

"What was her name?" Ellie asked gently.

Brittney swallowed, then looked at me, straight in the eye as she answered.

"Heather," she said.

chapter ten

my new friend, naomi

The Forest Grove waterpark opened on June 5, the day school let out, and after a few years, it'd become a family tradition to visit that refreshing sanctuary every year after school on that final day.

When school finally ended for the summer—ah, summer!—I sprang off the bus, looking forward to an afternoon of swimming and a summertime of fun. Before I got too far, however, Ellie grabbed my arm. "Faye! Hang out today to celebrate?"

"Ellie," I said, pulling away, "I'm going to the waterpark with my family like always. You know that."

"Well, can I come with?" Ellie said, as she always did. I sighed. "Ellie, I don't know why you're even asking. I mean, you already know the answer. My parents want it to be a family day. Besides, aren't you doing something with your family?"

Ellie scowled. "Just going out to dinner, but that's nothing special or out of the ordinary. There's nobody to see or talk to at the restaurants. At least you have siblings to chat with."

I raised my eyebrows. "Have you *met* my siblings?"

"No," said Ellie. "Tell me, what are their names?"

I tried to scowl at her, but instead only succeeded in laughing at her sarcasm.

"Seriously, Faye," said Ellie, then her face lit up. "Aha! I'll ask my parents if we can go to the waterpark, too! Then I'll see you there."

"Excellent idea," I agreed. "See you later, then?"

She grinned. "You betcha!" Then she turned and fled the opposite direction, towards her house. I shook my head, watching her, then ran back home.

•   •   •   •

We left for the park that afternoon. When we arrived, the parking lot was full of cars, as always. I searched the rows for Ellie's bright-blue car, but didn't find it; they either had parked in a separate lot, or they had decided not to come at all. Or maybe they were coming later on.

We waited anxiously in line for the attendant

to give us our admission bracelets. Walking through the gates, I took a deep breath and closed my eyes. I felt the spray on my face, and heard water flowing and dumping around me. One of the best feelings in the world. Today was going to be such a great afternoon.

Dad gathered us and explained the deal: first, we would do some rides together as a family, then we could split up, girls with Mom, Jack with Dad.

After a quick debate, the family decided on the tube slide first. Grabbing an inflated tube, I raced up the steps ahead of the others. "Faye," Mom called warningly, "wait up for us." I did, straying back a few steps to wait with Stella. The line wasn't too bad, five to ten minutes, maybe, but I didn't mind. I couldn't wait to feel the cool water envelop me.

Stella's tube bumped mine as she tried to get up the steps. "Sorry."

"Hey, it's okay," I said.

"Can I go first?" Stella asked.

Today I wasn't annoyed by her subtle-selfishness; I grinned, impressed with her boldness, and stepped down so she could get in front. "Go for it, Stel!"

She grinned, and held up her tube. "I'm gonna go so fast, you're not even going to see me!"

"Impossible," Jack said.

"That's great, Stel," I said, in no mood to let Jack's comments bother me and happy for my little sister's enthusiasm.

As we ascended, slowly but surely, I leaned

against the metal railing for the view. I could see everything from here: all the slides; the lazy river; the kiddie area; *everything*. People flocked the slides, and the pool was full of swimmers. I closed my eyes and listen to the water rushing. The air was a balmy 87 degrees, according to the car thermostat, and the water was surely cold. A nice change from the bitter winter weather for sure. I searched the swimmers for Ellie, but didn't have any success.

"Faye," Mom tapped me, breaking me from my thoughts.

"Yeah, what, Mom?"

"When you get the bottom, make sure you stay right there and wait for us, okay?" she said. "There's a lot of people here, and I don't want us to get separated."

I shrugged. "Okay."

I looked up to see Stella was about to go. The one person remaining ahead of her, a girl my age, smiled at Stella before sitting in her tube. She leaned back and gave herself a shove forward. Her tube rocketed down the dark tunnel, and we heard her shouts of delight echoing off the walls. I leaned over in time to see the tube shoot out the end. The girl, still thrilled, toppled off her tube and into the water. When she resurfaced, she was still grinning.

Stella had been watching, too. "I won't fall off, will I, Faye?" she asked me nervously.

"I don't think so," I reassured her. "Besides, even if you did, you're a good swimmer."

"Yeah." Stella, nervous and excited, mounted

her tube and whooshed down. I watched the end until she emerged, safe and sound, and still on her tube.

Excited for my turn, I set my float down and sat on it, grasping the handles firmly. After a moment's thought, I reached up and pulled my goggles down, intending to swim underwater right as I got out. Stella didn't think so, but for me, underwater was the best part of swimming.

I looked at the attendant to make sure I was clear to go, and felt her eyes taking in my scar. *I wish I didn't have a scar. Life would be so much easier.* I self-consciously bent my head lower, and then pushed forward, down into the darkness.

I torpedoed, whooping and screaming the entire way. The water swished up and mist sprayed my face. I laughed, delighted, the laugh echoing behind me as I tore down the slide. Then it was light again, and I rocketed into the water. Just for fun, I leapt off and half-swam underwater, half-dragged the float to the stairs, where I waited with Stella for Mom.

After a few more slides, all of which were as amazing as the first, the family decided to split up. Stella and I, wanting a few moments of calm, rushed to the lazy river with Mom hurrying after us, yelling for us to wait up. Dad and Jack headed to the high slide, the one we hadn't ridden because Stella was afraid.

At the lazy river, Stella and I both selected our floats and slid into the water. Without even trying to, I swiftly passed Stella, who was kicking her legs frantically in attempt to go faster.

"Faye!" Mom yelled, and I sighed in annoyance. "What, Mom?"

"You're getting too far ahead," Mom scolded me. "Wait up for me and your sister."

I made a face, but stopped moving and let the water current carry me along in the river. I sat peacefully, thinking, watching, while Mom hurried to catch up. I didn't know what it was with her these days and always having to know where I was. Pregnancy, I guessed. I spotted Jack and Dad in line at the high slide and smiled, knowing they'd be going back for a second round, soon. Jack was so daring like that.

I flashed back to the tube slide, where the attendant had stared at my scar. Almost involuntarily my fingers traced it, a straight line angled up on my left cheek.

The details of how I'd gotten such a scar were hazy. When I first asked about it at six years old, Mom simply said it was part who I was. I took that answer for granted for a long time. When I asked her again at age ten, knowing there was more to it than just that, she told me that I had cut myself with glass once and it never really healed right. I wasn't quite sure what to believe, anymore. Ellie had her whole list of theories of how it came about—one being a unicorn touched me as a baby and my skin couldn't handle the touch—but as for me, I let it be. Though I was curious, I didn't necessarily want to know if it was bad enough that Mom would never tell me. For a moment I remembered Brittney's story, that her sister, Heather, had died in a car crash, and had a fleeting thought that maybe a crash was also how I got my scar. But I shook it away; that was impossible, not to mention plain silly. Mom would have told me if I'd been in an accident!

I shook myself from my thoughts and lazily spun around in my tube. Stella was behind me, desperately trying to catch up. Mom was at her heels, yelling at me. "Faye, stop and wait for us."

I groaned, but skimmed my feet along the bottom and grabbed the side, stopping myself. Being six months pregnant made Mom much slower than normal, and I sat there anxiously by the side for quite a bit.

Finally, out of breath, Stella and Mom reached us. Mom, of course, yelled at me immediately. "Faye Corcoran, this is a big waterpark and you are only twelve years old. You'd better make sure you're with me from now on."

"Okay, Mom," I sighed, and eagerly kicked off from the wall, glad to be swimming again. But I was careful this time not to outdistance them.

A few minutes later, I heard laughter. I first thought it was Stella and looked around to see what was so funny. Instead, I saw two other kids.

A girl my age—I immediately recognized her as the one on the slide before us—and a boy a little younger. They were swimming rapidly ahead of me. The girl had short brown hair, dark eyes, and wore braces. The boy, with his own dark hair and eyes, was most likely her brother. His hair was long, and in his eyes, reminding me of Logan. He brushed it away as he tried to escape his sister; it looked like they were either racing or playing a form of tag.

The girl, breathless, spun around in her tube and bumped into mine. "Sorry!" she blushed. Her embarrassment didn't last long, however; her brother rammed his tube into hers from behind, and then she was off laughing and chasing him again.

Even though I doubted she'd hear me, I said, "It's fine." I scraped my feet along the bottom to avoid another collision, not that it'd be a big deal if we did collide.

After I had successfully stopped, I looked back at the two kids.

I watched in surprise as suddenly, the boy came forward and leapt out of his tube onto his sister's.

Screaming, but not in anger or annoyance, she shoved him off, and then splashed him for good measure. "Eli Richter, you are impossible!"

I watched, interested. The boy clambered back into his tube, then spun around and splashed his sister again. She laughed. Then they both seemed to notice they were blocking my way, and the girl's cheeks flushed as she said, "I'm sorry!"

"Hey, it's fine," I said, and looked around quickly. Stella and Mom were right behind me, and Mom gave us a friendly smile.

"What's your name?" I added, feeling friendly.

"Naomi," she said breathlessly, her brown eyes dancing. "That's my little brother. Eli."

Eli didn't seem to be listening, as he didn't say a greeting or anything polite. Naomi shook her head, sighing. "Brothers."

"It's fine," I found myself saying yet again, understanding because I had a brother much like that. "I'm Faye. Are you guys twins or something? You look alike."

"Really?" Naomi asked, laughing. "No, thank goodness! He's my little bro. Only eleven."

"How old are you?" I asked.

"Twelve. I turned twelve last week. You?"

"I'm twelve too," I said, liking Naomi more by the minute.

"What did you say your name was?" Mom said, getting into my business again. "I'm Faye's mom."

Naomi gave a wide grin. "I'm Naomi. Hi, Faye's mom."

I closed my eyes; at least Naomi was friendly. Didn't Mom understand that sometimes twelve-year-olds just needed to talk without their mother intervening?

"What are you girls gonna do?" Mom asked next.

I looked at Naomi. Naomi looked at me.

"Uh, Mom, we just met, like, five minutes ago," I said.

"Not even," Eli commented.

"Mom, I think we'll just stay here for now," I

said slowly.

"Well, okay then. Just let me know when you plan to leave," Mom replied.

I felt my cheeks flush; why couldn't Mom just leave us alone? "I'll tell you, Mom, if we do."

"Good. Okay, I'll leave you alone now."

Finally. I discreetly kicked a little harder to put a smidge more distance between us, and focused on Naomi. As we swam, we talked, and I found her a fun, energetic girl.

"So, here by yourself?" I asked her.

"No," she said, and pointed up ahead. "Eli's here, and my mom's somewhere around here."

"She lets you be on your own at the waterpark?" I said enviously.

"Yeah, pretty much," Naomi said.

"Lucky," I said.

"So," she said after a moment, "I know that's your mom. Who else is in your family?"

"Well, Stella's here, too," I said, pointing her out. "And my dad and my brother, too. They're probably on the most dangerous slide here."

She nodded, then paused and looked at me funny. "Wait. You look kind of familiar. Have I seen you before?"

I wished I could be as straightforward as her. "I think—I mean—we might have been—I think you were ahead of us in the tube slide line," I ventured.

"Oh, right!" Naomi said. "Don't you just love that slide? The speed, the dark, the water?"

I laughed. "It's one of my favorites."

"Me too."

We floated along together. The exit came along, but I decided to go another lap with my new friend.

Mom caught up to us, not that we had ever been far ahead of her. "Faye, how are you doing? Ready for anything else?"

Uncomfortably, I looked at Naomi. "I'll tell you when I'm ready, Mom."

"Yeah, I know, honey."

Stella floated along. "What are you talking about?"

"Random things."

The river flowed us along farther.

"Who's in your family?" I asked.

"Besides Eli? I've got a big sister named Lauren, but she's never home. And I've got a little sister, but she's only two," went on Naomi. "Ava. She's adorable but a lot of work."

I smiled. "I wish I had a little sister that age." Then I remembered. "Oh! I will soon. I mean, I could soon. My mom's pregnant."

"Really?" said Naomi. "That's awesome! Do you know if it's a boy or girl?"

Why did it seem like everyone was asking me that? I smiled. "My parents are going to let it be a surprise."

"Nice," she said, and smiled.

We kept floating along, talking, laughing. I was glad I'd met Naomi. I hadn't gotten to bring Ellie, and she'd never shown up, but it turned out maybe I was getting a friend along anyway. I liked Naomi. Maybe we could be friends. If she attended our school, then maybe our trio of Ellie, Logan, and me could become a quartet including Naomi.

"Where do you live?" I asked her.

"California," she responded. "We're just here on vacation."

My heart sank. "So you don't just...I mean...you don't live here?"

"No." Her face lit up. "But we should be pen pals!"

I'd never had a pen pal. "Awesome! Let's do it!"

Naomi smiled. Then she frowned and cocked her head. "You know, you look *really* familiar to me—except the scar. I mean, the person you remind me of doesn't have—"

"Faye, where did Jack and Dad go again?" Mom interrupted, swimming up to us as she looked around the waterpark. "My memory's all over the place today."

I sighed. "The Splash Coaster, Mom."

"Ah, right," Mom said. "Sorry, won't interrupt you again."

Yeah, right. I turned back to Naomi and opened my mouth, but not before Stella cried, "Faye, look!"

"What?"

"Jack," she said nervously. "He's trying to get me, I swear he is."

Why couldn't Naomi and me actually get to

the finish of a conversation without being constantly interrupted?

"Get you?" I repeated dubiously, shooting Naomi an *I'm-sorry* look. "What does that even mean?"

"He's creeping around, looking at me and holding a bucket," Stella accused.

I closed my eyes.

Naomi, thankfully, took over for me. "Don't worry," she said, and kindly patted Stella's head. Annoyed, Stella pushed the hand away, and I started to apologize, but Naomi waved it away. She laughed and said, "You're Stella, right? Well, this Jack kid won't dare mess with you. Don't worry. See, look, your mom is with us, plus I'm here and he wouldn't dare be so rude as to dump water on a complete stranger. Right, Faye?" she said, looking at me for clarification.

"Right," I said, smiling thankfully at her. "See, Stel, you have nothing to worry about." *Now leave us alone.*

Stella grumbled, but accepted our explanation.

The fun of the lazy river wore off soon, and we decided to go down the tube slide again, together. It'd only been twenty or so minutes, but already I'd felt like I'd known Naomi forever. Mom saw us getting out and hurried the best she could to follow. "Wait up, Faye!"

Naomi looked at Mom's stomach. "Wow, you're right, she *is* pregnant."

Mom seemed annoyed. "Faye, I told you to

wait for me when you decided to leave."

"No, you only told me to tell you," I said.

"Faye," she warned.

"Come on, Naomi, Stel." I trudged ahead; we reached the slide and got in line, not without Mom right on our heels. "Faye, I'm going to stay here and wait for you, okay? Don't talk to strangers, watch your sister and come right out once you reach the bottom."

"Man, your mom's harsh," Naomi said as we mounted the steps. She didn't say it in a rude tone; rather, similar to Ellie's style, she was more like commenting.

While we were in the line, Naomi and I chatted while Stella stood behind, silent.

"You can go first," Naomi graciously offered me when we reached the top.

"No, you can go," I said.

"You," she insisted.

"No, you," I said.

The attendant at the top seemed more and more annoyed with us with every "No, you!" Finally he said, "You, you go!" and pointed to Stella.

Embarrassed, Naomi and I stepped aside so Stella could get in her tube. Naomi nudged me. "We can't annoy him anymore. Then we'll get kicked out. So you just go."

I groaned good-naturedly. "*Fine.*"

The ride was as fun as the previous one. When we all got out, grinning and wet, we kept our tubes with us. "We *have* to do that again," Naomi said.

Our plans were cut short when suddenly a middle-aged woman, wearing regular clothes instead of a swimsuit, ran up to us with Eli reluctantly following her. Flustered, she took the tube from Naomi's hands and put it back in the pile. As she did so, she cried variations of *we're leaving this minute*, *I've been looking for you everywhere*, and *we've stayed an extra thirty minutes on accident and now we're running late*. Naomi protested, even going over to get her tube back, but the woman who was obviously her mother was firm. Firm and frantic. "Naomi Richter, we are running *extremely* late. Put that tube back. We are leaving right *now*." While Naomi slowly and reluctantly dragged the tube back, the woman spotted Stella and me. "Hello, dear," she said, her voice kind yet rushed. "Are you one of Naomi's friends? I don't believe we've met."

"Um—my name's Faye," I said, unsurely, not knowing what "friend" was defined as in her vocabulary but hoping I qualified. Naomi, fun, energetic and friendly, was one girl I hoped I could keep a friendship with—even if it was one through mail.

"Faye, huh?" she said, looking at me while Naomi reluctantly took the towel she was offered and wrapped herself up.

I felt uncomfortable under her gaze. "Yeah," I said while wondering where my own mother was.

Right as the thought entered my mind, Mom appeared behind me. "Faye, there you are." She looked at Naomi then at the woman. "Hello," she said wryly.

"Our daughters appear to be friends." The woman extended her hand. "Caroline Richter."

Mom hesitated for what seemed like too long before shaking and saying, "Kimberly Corcoran."

"Well," she said. "Good to meet you. Let's go, kids. Eli, get your feet out of the water. We don't have time for stalling. It's not getting any earlier."

"No, wait!" Naomi cried. "I have to give Faye my address so we can be pen pals!"

Her mom sighed. "Naomi, I don't have paper on me, much less pencil. I'm sorry, but that's the way things are."

I spun on my own mother, knowing the contents of her purse. "Mom, you have paper and pencil!"

Mom shook her head. "No time, Faye. We've gotta go, too."

"What? You said we would be here until five!"

"It's five now, Faye."

Naomi's mother said, "Four-thirty."

"Four-thirty, then. We're still leaving. We're going to Koz's."

Not even the thought of mashed potatoes cheered me up. "Mom, just one paper? I need to keep in touch!"

"Fine," Mom said, picking a notebook from her bag and thrusting it at me.

"Here." Naomi scribbled down hers, and I was picking up the pencil to do the same when Mom grabbed my arm. "One's enough. Come on, let's go. So long, Naomi."

"But—but—" I cried, to no avail. Finally I relented and yelled, "Bye, Naomi! I'll write, I promise!"

Then everything went dark.

chapter eleven

green eyes

Okay, not legitimately dark. A bucket was on my head, formerly filled with water. Not that I wasn't wet already, but now I was drenched.

Furious, I pulled the bucket off my head to find Jack, doubled over, laughing like it was the funniest thing in the world.

"Ha, ha, very funny, Jackson Smith!" I yelled, then bent down to scoop some water to throw in his face—he deserved it—but then I spotted a soggy piece of paper with blurred markings on it slowly shriveling up and starting to sink. "No! You rotten boy, you ruined my only chance to keep in touch with Naomi!" I threw the bucket at him and then grabbed the page delicately from the water. It was soaked through, however, and the page fell apart in my hands. The words that remained had been smudged and blurred into illegibility. In despair, I looked to Mom for guidance, who didn't seem the least sorry for me. "Oh, Faye, that's too bad. Jackson Corcoran, please watch your behavior."

Jack almost seemed regretful. "Aw, Faye, it's not like you'll ever actually see her again."

"Go away, Jack!" Stella shouted.

"Glad to." Jack stooped, picked his bucket, and then stalked off.

"Jackson!" Mom yelled after him. "This conversation is not over!" But the way she said it made me wonder if it was.

•　　•　　•　　•

Summer wore on, hot and humid. I got together with Ellie and Logan often, and most of those times, we ended up in one of our backyards, spraying each other with the hose, battling out in water gun fights, or playing water balloon games. Stella occasionally joined us, but Jack never did—he was always gone, out somewhere partying. Or something like that. I never really knew where he went, only that Mom said he was "with friends."

Besides that, my new baby sibling was really starting to make itself known; by the end of June, there was no denying my mother was expecting. It created an excited atmosphere in my house; all in all, there was less bickering and more smiles.

By July, we were counting down the days (actually, it was Stella counting, and occasionally I encouraged her by asking how many days remained), despite the fact that Mom had told us, over and over, that there was a very slim chance that the baby would actually arrive on the due date.

One afternoon, Ellie was over when Stella came up with a slightly brilliant, "secret" idea.

When Ellie and I, sitting in my room and chatting, first heard Stella's knock, we thought it was Brittney (it was Friday).

"The cleaning lady invades!" Ellie cried. "Hurry, get under the bed and hide!"

I laughed, and got up to answer the door. When I opened it, I was surprised by Stella waiting there, rather than Brittney, who'd we'd thought. "Oh! Stel, it's just you."

"Who else would I be?" she asked. "Jack never knocks, you know that." She giggled, and looked both ways before adding, "And Mom's too fat to climb the stairs."

"Stella!" I said.

But Ellie, having overheard, was laughing. "What's wrong, Fayster? Stellie's right, ain't she?"

"My name's *Stella*," Stella said indignantly.

"No," I answered Ellie's question, "her bedroom's up here. And she sleeps up here."

"My mistake," said Ellie, and her attention returned to Stella. "So, Stell-O Girl-O, what's up?"

Stella scowled. "Ellie!"

"Stella!"

I sighed. "Both of you, calm down. Stella, what did you need?"

Stella lowered her voice. She closed the door, then said, "I came to see if you have ideas."

"Ideas? About what?" For a fleeting moment, I thought she was going to bring up a Brittney-based idea like one of Ellie's, but then she said instead, "To help Mom. I mean, the baby's due really soon, Faye. And she's really cranky. We should do something to help her."

"She's totally right!" Ellie exclaimed, jumping up suddenly. "Isn't she, Fayster?"

"Huh?"

"We need to do something to help your mom." Ellie leapt off the bed and proceeded to pace around the interior of my room. "What could it be? What could it be?"

I had a few vague ideas of my own, but I kept my mouth shut, and watched her pace, knowing soon enough she'd come up with some brilliant plan that we'd all have to follow.

Sure enough, before long she jumped up: "Faye, what will the baby wear?"

"What?"

"Where will the clothes mainly come from?" The tone of her voice told me she already knew the answer.

Knowing this, I didn't say anything and waited for her to answer her own question, which, of course she did. "If it's a girl, she'll use your and

Stella's hand-me-downs—right? And if it's a boy, she'll use Jack's. Am I right?"

"Mostly, but Jack's sixteen. We probably don't have much of his anymore."

Ellie ignored me. "And how tired is your mom these days?"

"Um, really tired?" I tried, not knowing where she was going with it.

"Will she have time to go downstairs, sift through all the old clothes, to find good ones?"

I realized where she was going. "Great idea, Ell. Let's go."

"Wait!" Stella cried as she followed us out the door. "What are we doing?"

I instantly shushed her, figuring she'd know sooner than later, keeping the project secret. I crept through the family room, leading Ellie and Stella. Brittney was in the kitchen, scouring the counters, while Mom sat at the table, drinking coffee again. "Hello, girls," Brittney greeted us.

Mom echoed, "Hello, girls. What are you up to?"

Just heading down to the basement for a bit," I said casually, hoping that that didn't sound too suspicious. But Mom just said, "Be careful down there, and don't go in the storage room, okay?" She shook her head. "I need to get down there to organize that mess sometime soon."

Ellie and I exchanged private, guilty smiles. The storage room, where the baby clothes were, was exactly where we were headed.

The basement door creaked as we opened it; the carpet on the stairs was fuzzy and soft beneath our feet as we descended downstairs.

Our basement was finished, but there was a section off the living-room area, closed off by a door, that wasn't finished. Mom called it the storage room, but thanks to Ellie, I never called it that.

"Come on." Silently, I pushed the door open to the room, full to the brim with boxes. "Should we pull them out?" I called to Ellie, who had gotten distracted again by something on the stairs. "There's not enough room in the creepy room to actually do any work in there," I added, using the nickname Ellie had given the room. I didn't agree completely with the name, since it didn't creep me out, but when your best friend uses a nickname all the time, it's impossible not to catch onto the habit.

Ellie finally had made her way behind me. "Let's just pull them outside into the living room, then. But only one box at a time."

"Good idea," I said. "Okay, Ellie, Stel, ideas? We need a quick, believable reason for being in there and messing with boxes if Mom happens to come down."

"She won't," Stella said. "She's too tired."

I ignored her, but Ellie said, "Actually, Faye, I think we'll be okay without one. Stel is kind of right. I don't think your mom will actually come down here unless, you know, we start screaming or something."

"Okay," I relented reluctantly. "Let's get

started then."

Ellie and I stepped inside to lift the first box. The cement floor was cold. The small light bulb provided very little relief from the darkness, and the towers of boxes loomed over us. Ellie tapped the one closest to us. "This one."

I slipped my hands under it. "Stel," I whispered urgently, "come help us."

Silently we managed to get the box out of the room. I opened the flaps. "Success!" Inside the box were girls' clothes, and they looked small.

Ellie peered at the side of the box. "Your clothes, to be exact."

"Really?" I started lifting tiny, old items of clothing out of the box and laying them on the carpet. "I was a small baby."

"Guess you were," Ellie giggled. "Okay, let's form three piles as we go through them: yes, definitely-no, and maybe."

"Good idea." I picked up a striped onesie. "I really wore this?"

•　　•　　•　　•

Twenty minutes later, we had dug through the entire box plus two others, and our piles were growing, though the 'yes' pile was by far the smallest. Most of the items were stained, ripped, or otherwise smelly and old from being in boxes; Mom, it seemed, hadn't come down here in practically years.

"What's this?" Ellie asked, looking into the last box and then lifting out two dusty, thick photo albums. "They were buried under all the clothes."

I took one, dusted it off, and looked at the inscription on the front: *Corcoran kids: Jackson, 2nd-3rd grade; Faye, K-1st grade; Stella, 0-24 months.*

"Aww, this is when you were little!" Ellie said, reading the words as well, and snatched the book off my lap. "I *have* to see this."

"Ellie…" I sighed.

"Me too!" Stella said eagerly and dashed over beside Ellie.

Ellie started flipping the pages. "Awwww, look at this, Faye!" She pointed at one in which a little Jack, probably age seven, sits with a little blonde-haired child—me—on his lap.

"Where am I?" Stella asked.

"You weren't born yet, Stel." Ellie continued to flip through.

The way they were sitting together reminded me of the picture of Brittney and her sister, but I brushed it away from my mind, not wanting to think about it now.

"Oh, just *look* at you!" Ellie said. "You guys are *soooo* cute."

Suddenly, something caught my eye, and I stopped Ellie's flipping by putting my finger on the page. "Wait, what's that on my face?"

Ellie bent over. "Where?"

"Right there." I frowned, utterly confused.

"There's a mark on my cheek."

Ellie frowned, too, and looked at me, puzzled. "It looks like a birthmark. Is that the same cheek you have your scar?"

I looked. "No, it's the other one."

"Hmm." Ellie looked at it again. "I think it's just a smudge. These photos are really old."

I looked at it, and said, "Yeah, I think you're right. Hmm. Funny, though."

We continued looking through the album. Eventually, a baby appeared in the pictures: Stella, which delighted my now-eight-year-old sister.

Then we came to a page featuring three individual pictures of us: Jack, age eight and in third grade, wearing a blue T-shirt, his hair combed back and a cheesy grin on his face.

Stella was next in line, barely a few months old. Dressed in a pink shirt and fluffy pink skirt, she lays on a purple surface, her eyes squeezed shut; a thin pink band with a flower on it encircles her tiny head.

"Oh! Look at you, Stel! You're just soooo cute!" Ellie cried, clasping her hands together. "Your style hasn't changed one bit! I guess you were just born wearing wild, weren't you? Don't you still have that skirt?"

Stella scowled, hating being referred to as "cute," and folded her arms. "I'm going to get a snack."

Nobody stopped her from stomping upstairs; we both knew eight-year-olds, especially Stella, couldn't go too long without a snack.

My eyes traveled back to the page to find me.

I'm in first grade, barely, in the picture, because the caption reads, *Faye, age 5.* My light blonde hair is thin and straight—funny, considering how thick and curly it was now—and adorned by a sparkly blue headband. I'm wearing a green shirt with a pink heart necklace, and my eyes, bright and green, are cheerful and match my enthusiastic smile.

"Ooooh, you're *so* cute, Faye!" said Ellie. "Just look at you. Man, I wish I'd known you when you were five. By the time we met, you had just outgrown your cuteness."

I stuck my tongue out at her, and she laughed, but I didn't laugh along. There was something about the picture that was bothering me.

"What is it, Fayster?"

"Firstly, Ell," I said, "I don't think that was a smudge."

The marking was on my cheek, the same mark we'd seen previously, right there plain as day. In the same manner, my would-be scarred cheek was turned away from the camera; I couldn't tell if there was a scar there or not, but it didn't look like it.

The silence echoed in the room around us.

"That is really mysterious, Faye," Ellie said, running her finger along the picture. "Are we sure the pictures aren't just all old and smudgy?"

"All of them?" I pointed out. "And they're not *that* old."

Ellie shook her head and flipped the page.

"It's here, too. Look."

Anxiously, we went through the whole book; every picture of me had the mark, and none of them had the scar.

"Well, I'm confuffled," said Ellie.

I didn't even bother to ask; from time to time, Ellie found it necessary to invent her own words.

Finally, Ellie leaned back and said, "There's a strange mark on your face when you're five, and it looks like there's no scar. Now, you're twelve, there's no mark but there is a scar. Confuffling, isn't it?"

"What *is* it, even? The mark?"

Ellie picked up the book and held it to her face. "I think it's a birthmark," she finally announced. "Aha! That's gotta be it. That would make the most sense. Because then, your parents could have had it removed."

"Maybe that's where the scar came from," I said.

"You said yourself it's the wrong cheek."

"Yeah, I know," I responded absently.

Ellie was quiet. Then she said seriously, "My third-cousin had a birthmark like that once, Faye, but they had to remove it because it was infected."

"Birthmarks can be infected?" I said.

"It was the start of a scary, terrible, fatal, awful disease," Ellie went on. "So they took it off, and now she's all better."

"For real, Ellie?"

"Well, probably. Anyway, I bet that's what

happened to yours, and your mom never told you because when she thinks of the birthmark she thinks of that awful, horrible disease, and that makes her scared, so she doesn't tell you so she doesn't have to think about it."

"Sure, Ellie, I'm sure that's it," I said sarcastically, and traced the profile of my sweet, five-year-old face. Chills raced up my spine and suddenly, I felt very uneasy.

"Ellie," I said. "My eyes are blue."

"Yeah, so what?"

"Ellie, they're green in this picture."

Stomping on the stairs interrupted our conversation and within moments Stella appeared. She came and sat next to us, still chewing. When she saw we were still looking at the albums, she made a face. "Still?"

"Yeah, still." Ellie looked at me funny, still contemplating my words, and then said, "Well, maybe it's not you, then. Maybe it's Stella."

"Huh?" Stella looked up, but we ignored her.

"Then who's the baby?" I said, unable to rid myself of the uneasiness.

"Maybe it's Jack, then," Ellie suggested playfully. "The baby could be you."

I stared at her, not at all in the mood for jokes.

Stella, on the other hand, grinned and crossed her arms. "Then who's the other boy?"

Ellie sheepishly looked at the floor.

"And second," Stella said, "when, when, when have you ever seen Jack in a dress? Because if you have, I need to know: one, when was this strange occasion, and two, why wasn't I apart of it?"

"Stel," groaned Ellie.

"What?" Stella said. "And what are we talking about, anyways?"

"There's a mysterious smudge-thing or birthmark, one of the two anyway, on Faye's cheek in every single picture of Faye in this book, and there's no scar," Ellie explained. "Any ideas?"

"A smudge?" Stella repeated.

"Birthmark or something." I shoved the album at her. "See? But I don't have one now."

Stella's eyes drifted from the pictures to me. "What? Of course you do!" Stella leaned over and pushed the hair off my face to see, and I angrily shoved her hand away. "Satisfied? Stella, I don't *ever* remember having a birthmark."

Stella shrugged. "So what? Maybe they, like, removed the birthmark, and then the scar was what was left."

"Wrong!" Ellie said. "It's the opposite cheek."

"Oh." Stella shrugged again. "Well, maybe it just faded away. I mean, look. Your hair was blonde then, and now it's brown. Same way, I bet birthmarks can just fade away as you get older, just like hair."

I shook my head. "Birthmarks can't just disappear, Stella. They have to be—I don't know—removed or something."

"So, you got it removed then," Stella said nonchalantly.

Ellie nodded. "Exactly," she said. "It was the start of a cancerous disease."

"What?" Stella said, crinkling her nose in confusion.

"Ellie's exaggerating," I explained.

"No, I'm not," Ellie contradicted me.

Stella shrugged. "Either way, what's the big deal? We can just ask Mom when we go upstairs."

"Then she'll know what we've been doing," I cried. "This is supposed to be a surprise!"

"Well—we don't have to tell her exactly," Stella said. "We can just tell her, I don't know, we were playing down here and stumbled upon them."

"Stumbled upon boxes that were stacked in piles inside the creepy room? And since when do we 'play' in the basement?" The green-eye thing was still bothering me, and I couldn't shake the strange feeling…it scared me.

"I did," Stella mumbled, "last year for my birthday."

"Key word: *last year*," Ellie said.

"What?" Stella said.

"Key word, *birthday*," Ellie said.

"Key word, *I did*," Stella shot back.

"Key word, *we're down here now*," Ellie replied.

"Key word, *now*," Stella said.

"Key word, *birthday cake*," Ellie said.

Stella stopped. "What?"

"I'm being silly. Go with it."

"Key word: *Cookies*."

"Key word: *Fruit punch*."

"Key word: *Brownies*!"

This went on for a while. The uneasiness hadn't left me yet; there was something off about this, but something I couldn't nail down. It was the same feeling I'd had when I picked up the picture. The picture…Sudden feelings surged through me and I turned to my best friend and sister.

"Key word: Why are we saying 'key word'?" I cried, interrupting. "You guys don't make *any* sense. Let's just hope she doesn't come down here, okay? Come on, Ellie, let's go get another box."

"Key word: *hope*," Ellie said.

"Ellie!"

"Key word: *sorry*!"

"Ellie, please," I said.

"Sorry, Faye," she said.

●　　●　　●　　●

An hour later, I walked up the basement stairs, one step at a time, feeling my way carefully with my feet because my arms were piled high with yes-pile clothing to surprise Mom with—after we washed it, of course. Originally we'd wanted to wait a little while, but, as Ellie ingeniously pointed out, it would be mysterious if Mom happened to stumble upon a bunch of piles of clothing in the basement. It worked out good, because this way we could ask about the photo albums, too, and the strange mark on my cheek.

Behind me, Ellie followed, her arms also heaped with clothes, except hers were the maybe pile. Behind her was Stella, with the smallest pile by far. She'd wanted to carry the no-pile, but it was too big to lug in one trip, so we'd agreed to go back down later. As a result, Stella was stuck with the leftover-yeses and maybes, and was complaining about how tiny it was. Tired, I had dumped the photo albums on top of her pile to make her seem like it was bigger.

Still, she was grumbling, something about how she got the "small" pile and how, somehow, that meant we were treating her as a baby and how "sick she was of it."

"Stel," I said, struggling as I tried to reach for the doorknob, "I did give you the photo books. Count it as a bonus."

"Faye speaks the truth," declared Ellie.

Stella continued to pout as we hauled the stuff upstairs: clothes of all style and color, as well as gender, as, of course, we didn't know if the baby was a boy or girl yet.

"So, Faye, I'm trusting you know how to work the washing machine?" Ellie whispered to me.

I looked at her. "No," I said. "Do you?"

"Out of luck," she whispered back. "Stel, do you?"

"Do I what?"

"Know how to work the washing machine?"

"Um, maybe," Stella said.

I sighed. "Let's ask Brittney," I said, figuring she worked around the house and, being a house-cleaner, probably knew how to do such a thing.

Of course, my suggestion thrilled Ellie. "Yes! Let's!"

Mom was sleeping on the couch upstairs. We snuck by her, holding the piles, and went into the front room; Brittney was scrubbing down the windows. It was 3:40, so she was getting ready to leave soon, probably.

Ellie tiptoed up and tapped Brittney's shoulder. When Brittney turned around, Ellie opened her eyes wide and said in a whisper, "Can you help us, Brittney?"

"With what?" she asked.

Ellie looked at me. "Me and Faye—"

"And me," Stella jumped in.

"And Stella. Me and Faye and Stella went downstairs and sorted all these baby clothes for Faye's mom, you know, a surprise, but they're all really musty and smelly and none of us know how to use the washing machine. Can you help us?"

Brittney looked at us and uttered a quick laugh. "You don't know?"

"No," I said, feeling embarrassed.

Brittney shook her head. "It's no problem, honestly. Come on, I'll help you guys. Is your...is your mom sleeping, Faye?"

"Yeah, which is why we have to do it now."

"Of course." Brittney set down her supplies quietly and we silently followed her into the laundry room.

Carefully and quietly, Brittney led us through step-by-step, of getting clean clothes. When the machine was finally started, she looked at us and said, "Well, now you know how. As for the dryer, all you have to do is load it in and press 'start.' Okay?"

We nodded, and left the room; we had thirty minutes until the load was finished. The hard part would be keeping Mom out of the laundry room until it was washed and dried, but it ended up not being a problem. Mom napped for a while longer, and when she woke up, she was only interested in having a cup of tea and reading a book.

An hour later, the washing and drying was finally finished.

"What now?" Ellie asked. Then she stopped. "Faye, where is this baby gonna sleep?"

I was startled. "I—I don't know," I stammered.

"Well, we can't put the clothes somewhere we don't know," Stella said. "Let's just present the clothes to Mom and ask her." Suddenly her face went somber. "I'm not sharing with you, Faye, even if the baby is a girl."

I hadn't even thought of that possibility. "I agree with Stel. Come on, let's just get the clothes and give them to Mom."

•   •   •   •

My mother was startled when she saw us.

"Girls," she said, then wiped her brow. "Where'd you find this stuff?"

Ellie and I exchanged guilty looks. "The creepy room," Stella said for us. "I know you said not to, but look at what we did for you!" Excited, she smiled proudly.

Mom looked anything but excited. "Well," she finally said. "That was lovely of you girls. But don't go down there again, you hear me, Faye?"

"What?" I was surprised; I'd expected her to be a lot more emphatic over it, rather than edgy.

"I don't want you guys in the creepy room," she said. "There's stuff down there...dangerous tools and things."

All I'd seen was boxes, but I didn't argue.

Ellie looked at me uncomfortably.

"We won't, Mom," I said, and then quickly changed the subject. "Where is the baby gonna sleep, Mom? We're out of bedrooms."

Mom gave a small smile. "We've thought of that, Faye. I think we're going to have to either put you and Stella together—"

"No!" Stella and me chimed together.

"—or convert Dad's office into a bedroom, and put Jack or someone down there. We aren't sure on the details."

"If you do change the office," I said, "I call it."

"No fair," Stella said. "I should get it. I'm the youngest."

"Girls, stop," Mom said, and sighed, looking

at the clock. "Goodness, it's already five-fifteen. Faye, please walk your friend home. Stella, please come help me with the kitchen. Jack is at Iain's house until dinner, so you're gonna have to do his chores."

While Stella pouted and complained, I slipped on my sandals and opened the door for Ellie, who was unusually quiet. "Hey, are you okay?" I asked her.

"Yeah," she said as we walked down the drive. "Your mom didn't even say goodbye to me."

"I'm sorry," I said. "She's really cranky. Pregnancy, you know."

"Yeah, I know," she said.

Our walk home was silent.

$$\bullet \quad \bullet \quad \bullet \quad \bullet$$

Over dinner, Stella, who, of course, never forgot about certain things, decided to take matters into her own hands.

"Mom?" she said.

Mom turned. "What, sweetie?" Her voice was tired and worn out.

"What happened to Faye's birthmark?"

I turned suddenly. "Stella!" I wailed.

Mom was suddenly alert, too. "What do you mean?" she asked sharply.

"We found some old photo albums," Stella

insisted. "Of like, you know, Faye when she was little. She has a mark-smudgy-thingy on every picture of her. But now—" Stella found it again necessary to reach across the table and shove my side bangs off my face. "See, she doesn't have it anymore," she said and I shoved her hand away once again.

Mom gripped the edge of the table. "Where did you find those photo books?" she said.

"When we were looking for—you know—the clothes."

Mom just looked at her. "In the storage room?"

"Yep. So, what happened to it?" Stella pressed, and then promptly stuck a forkful of pasta in her mouth.

Nonchalantly, Mom delivered the most significant sentence in my life. "It was removed after the crash." She avoided our eyes, her eyes on her food as she wound and unwound pasta around her fork.

"Crash?" Stella said, scrunching up her nose.

"Crash?" Jack said, lifting his eyebrows, who'd just gotten home from his friend's.

"Crash?" I exclaimed, blinking in confusion.

"The crash. The accident," Mom clarified and, still not meeting our eyes, took a long sip of her tea. When she finally looked up, she found all three of us staring at her.

Dad looked at her, too, but not in bewilderment. By his look, I could tell he already knew what she was talking about. So both of them knew.

Something they'd kept from me my whole life.

chapter twelve
birthmark vs. scar

Mom sighed, and exchanged a look with Dad. "I was hoping to wait, until you were older," she said testily, looking at us carefully. "We didn't want—I mean—okay, never mind. Might as well just start from the beginning and get it over with." She set down her mug with a clang, and then looked at me, right at me. "Faye, I'm sorry I never told you. When you were five years old, we were in a bad car accident. A crash, rather. A terrible wreck."

I just kept looking at her, wondering if this was a dream.

"You...ah, how do I say this. You barely made it out alive. When you got the hospital, there was already a lot to be done, and they decided just to remove the birthmark while you there." Apparently done with the story, Mom took a large sip of her tea, took a breath, and resumed eating. "And that's what happened to your birthmark, Faye."

I wondered how she could eat so calmly. My stomach was anything from calm; my appetite had disappeared completely. Absently I traced my cheek, the scar-less, smooth one, and double-checked what I knew: my scar was on my left cheek. In the picture, the birthmark was on the right.

My mind reeling over all the information I'd been given in the past two minutes, I fingered one cheek, and then the other. "Wouldn't there be a scar, though?"

"Excuse me?"

"If they removed the birthmark." I wasn't feeling so good anymore. "Wouldn't there be a scar on my face?"

Mom looked at me funny, as if something was wrong with me. "Honey, you *do* have a scar on your face."

I suddenly realized what I'd said and felt embarrassed, but pushed further. "No, it was on the opposite cheek."

"What? Nonsense," Mom said. "Faye, sweetie, it's the same. That's where you got your scar from."

"You said I cut myself with glass," I said. The uneasy feeling returned from earlier, and I pushed my plate away. "I want to know what's going on."

Mom looked at a loss, then she said, "I'm sorry, sweetie. The scar was pretty much all because of the accident. When you were young, it was just…well…easier to just say you cut yourself, rather than explaining." She stuck a forkful of food in her mouth, then took a drink and put her cup down hard, sloshing the tea onto the table.

Jack suddenly put his fork down abruptly. "So basically, what you're saying is, Faye was in this horrible, awful, traumatic car wreck—one which, by the way, I hardly remember—and got this awful scar, and then they bring her to the hospital and then decide to remove the birthmark while she's in there?"

Mom just looked at him, at a loss.

"Don't talk to your mother that way," Dad warned.

Ignoring Dad, Jack went on. "And you know what else is very mysterious? That she comes home and then *Bam!* all the photo books of us as little kids before the accident are hidden away. That's pretty creepy, don't you think? Maybe that's why we call it the creepy r—"

"Jackson Corcoran!" Dad said. "That's enough!"

"They were in a box," Stella cried, defending herself and her brother. "Under all the old clothes."

"That's very mysterious," Jack continued sarcastically. "And know what else is a really big coincidence? That right when Faye comes into the hospital after being a car wreck she barely survives, it happens to be *just* the right time to remove the birthmark, even though, you know, she's barely surviving."

"Jack—" Dad started.

"And know what else's really *funny*?" Jack said. "That the birthmark is the opposite cheek as her scar, which means there's no proof the birthmark even *existed*." He paused for a minute. "And then *where*, tell me, did the scar come from?" he drawled.

Abruptly, Mom got up from the table. She threw her napkin down and shoved her chair in. She silently walked upstairs, and I heard her door slam.

Dad closed his eyes. "Jackson Corcoran, enough is enough! The accident's a very hard thing for your mother to talk about. It was a very traumatic time for her."

"I'm sorry, Dad." He didn't seem sorry at all to me. "It just doesn't make any sense."

"I hope you enjoyed that little act of yours, because you're grounded," Dad said harshly, getting up from the table. "In fact, I don't even want you around. Why don't you go upstairs to your room?"

Jack flashed a cheesy grin. "Great, that means no chores!" He leapt from the table and dashed upstairs, slamming the door in his wake.

Dad shook his head. "Come help me clean up, girls," he said, and I followed, still feeling blinded from everything I'd learned.

chapter thirteen
remember the gingerdoodle

In my dreams, normally there was screaming. In this one, someone was laughing. Mom was in the front seat of the car, except she didn't look like Mom. Her hair was dark instead of blonde, and her eyes were dark, too. She looked out of the window of the car and I did, too, seeing it was smashed. Outside, an ambulance sat on the side of the road, its sirens wailing. Mom laughed again and said to me, "Faye, when you were five years old, you were in a bad car accident."

I woke to birds twittering outside my window. Opening my eyes, I found my room bright with morning sunlight. The peace comforted me, reminding me once again that dreams were only dreams and the wreck was only a dream, too.

No—suddenly, I was wide-awake. The crash

wasn't just a dream. I really had been in one, and Mom had never told me.

I absently wondered if she'd ever have told me, if we had never brought it up. One thing was sure: I never would have remembered it on my own. I always had assumed my dreams were just, well, dreams. I thought now that maybe they were memories my self-conscious had forgotten. Maybe it had been so traumatizing, the events had been blocked from my memory. I shivered at the mere thought. I was *glad* I didn't remember.

Footsteps sounded on the stairs, and the door to my room creaked open to reveal Mom on the phone with someone. "Yeah, she's just—Faye! Good morning!" she said brightly when she saw me awake. "Ellie's on the phone," she mouthed, and handed it to me.

I took the phone, shaking the remains of the dream, and pressed it to my ear. "Hi, Ell."

She laughed, a cheerful, welcome noise. "What's with the sleepiness?"

"I just woke up, literally, ten seconds ago," I said. Knowing my conversation was secure, Mom silently left the room.

"Whoops! Sorry, Faye!"

I rubbed my eyes, trying to drain away the sleepiness. "Well, what is it?"

"D'ya wanna come over today?" she asked excitedly. "Mom says we can do some baking if we want. We just got a new mixing-thingy machine! And we have ingredients for almost any—"

"What time?" I interrupted, cheerful at the prospect of seeing her.

"Anytime," she said cheerfully, then added, "Whoops, forgot you're still half asleep! Whenever you wake up."

"Will do," I answered. "See you in a bit."

"Bye," she said. "Wait, you need to tell me when—"

Knowing she would go on forever if permitted, I hung up. I collapsed on my bed, ever so grateful for Ellie.

After a little while, I finally got myself out of bed. I was tempted to wait hours before going to Ellie's, just to spite her, but baking sounded like a really good idea.

I rummaged through my closet before finding a t-shirt Ellie called my BFF shirt. A year or so ago, we'd gotten together to decorate matching shirts. We'd painted random things with puffy paint, and then gone to school and gotten a ton of people to sign them. Needless to say, Ellie came up with *that* idea. I didn't even know who the majority of the people who signed it were, but I had to admit, it looked pretty cool, covered in signatures.

I put it on along with a pair of jean shorts. I ran my fingers through my hair, pulled it into a ponytail, and then left my room.

Downstairs, I poured myself a bowl of cereal and started eating. Across the table, Mom looked up from her sketch. "Morning, honey."

"Morning."

"What did Ellie have to say?"

"She wants me to go over there later."

"Well, that's fine by me." Mom's eyes moved along the page as she worked. It was comforting, somehow, to see her working. Eight months pregnant made her more tired and worn out; only occasionally did she have the energy to do her work. That's what she told us, anyway. A few weeks ago, I'd overheard her and Dad talking and found out it was doctor's orders to go easy. Something about a high-risk pregnancy. I hadn't paid much attention, but I found it interesting.

The good news was, since she only worked part-time, as well owned the business with Dad, her work hours were a lot more flexible. She could work from home when it was needed, which it was a lot recently with her pregnancy and everything. Now, seeing her working told me she was feeling better. Most days I came down to breakfast and found her lying or sleeping on the couch.

"I'll go over there after breakfast, then. Is that okay?" I asked.

"Sure, honey. We'll call if we need you." Her eyes followed me as I finished up my cereal, then slipped on my shoes. "I'll be back later," I said, bidding her goodbye.s

"Where'you going?" a sleepy-eyed Stella called from the stairs, still in her pajamas. "Can I come, too?"

"Just to Ellie's," I called back, holding the door half-open. "And no, Stel, it's just me and Ellie this time. I'll see you later, though."

"Wait!" she called as I started closing the door. "If I get dressed right now, can I come?"

"No, Stel," I said, irritated, then sighed. "I'll bring you back some of whatever we bake." Before she could protest, I shut the door and proceeded down the steps. A knock on the window made me turn around to see Mom and Stella waving, and I rolled my eyes, waving back. I turned and resumed my walk, feeling just a bit more less free knowing Mom was watching to "make sure I got there".

The summer air was beautiful today: warmer than normal, but definitely not hot. The walk to Ellie's was about five minutes, and I enjoyed the few minutes alone, just taking in the gloriousness of summer.

When I got to Ellie's I didn't even need to knock. The door opened right up. "Faye, finally, you're here!" Ellie squealed.

I grinned. "Finally? It's barely been a half hour since your call."

Ellie grinned back at me, too. "I knew you'd be anxious to get over here, so I've been watching for you since."

I smiled. That was so like Ellie.

"Come on," she said, grabbing my hand. "Let's go bake up something yummy!"

Ellie's mom, Mrs. Anderson, was in the kitchen, wiping down the counters apparently in preparation for the mess we planned to make. "Why, hello, Faye! And how are you this morning?"

"I'm doing great, Mrs. Anderson," I responded politely. "How are you?"

"Thank you for asking, Faye. I'm doing quite well, actually. I'm looking forward to whatever treat you two cook up." She winked at me and deposited the wet rag in the sink.

Ellie made a face. "See how hard we work here, Faye? Mom, Faye's cleaning lady does *all* the dirty work. Faye has *no* chores to do. Ever."

"Ellie!" I cried, but I was laughing. "That is so not true!"

Mrs. Anderson chuckled, too. "So, what does this 'Brittney' do?"

"Dusting, vacuuming, that sort of stuff," I said. "And Ellie's partly right. She does do the dirty work. Yesterday she cleaned the inside of the fridge. She does it well, too," I hastened to add.

Mrs. Anderson nodded. "That's great, Faye. How often is she at your house?"

"Uh, Mondays, Wednesdays, Fridays," I said.

"Hmm. Very interesting. Ellie, why don't you go get my big cookbook from the cabinet, and then you and Faye can start destroying my kitchen." She smiled at us, and we laughed.

I followed Ellie into the foyer to get the cookbook from the cabinet, like her mom had said. After retrieving it, Ellie plopped it down on the counter. "Let's make something cold."

"Cold?" I said. "Aren't baked treats normally hot?"

"Well, we can freeze them." Ellie flipped

through the pages. "Ooh, don't these brownies look soooo good? We *have* to make them."

"Frozen brownies?" I said doubtfully.

"Why not?" she said.

"Ellie, it'll take hours to freeze," I pointed out, "and besides, don't you want to be able to eat them right out of the oven?"

"Oh. Guess you're right. Hot brownies it is," Ellie said cheerfully, abandoning her idea of something cold. Loudly, she started clanging all our tools down on the counter: the bowl, the metal whisk, a spatula, measuring cups and spoons, while I got out the ingredients.

Ellie dumped her third cup of flour into the bowl and then suddenly looked worried. "We need three cups, right, Faye?"

I checked the recipe and kept my face straight. "Nope, only two."

Then I burst out laughing at the stricken look upon her face. "I'm kidding, Ell. Three cups is perfect."

"Aw, Faye!" Ellie chucked her measuring cup into the sink, where it landed with an echoing clang. "You really had me there! Cut it out!" For good measure, she thrust a small handful of leftover flour at me.

"What!" I cried, brushing the white from my clothes and then throwing my own handful of flour at her.

Within minutes a flour fight had been engaged, and the baking abandoned.

Our battle cries and laughter brought Mrs. Anderson to the kitchen. When she entered, we froze, caked in white along with most of the kitchen.

"Elisabeth Madilyn Anderson," she cried, and Ellie's face went whiter; nobody ever used her full name unless she was truly in trouble. I felt a sickening guilt as I looked at Mrs. Anderson.

However, to my surprise, Mrs. Anderson started to laugh. "My goodness, Elisabeth, what else could I expect from you? I'll tell you what I'm going to expect, though. This kitchen spotless by tonight. Do you understand?"

Ellie nodded numbly.

"And, Ellie," Mrs. Anderson added, "no more food fights. I'd rather not have egg, milk, and sugar plastered all over my kitchen."

"Okay, Mom," Ellie murmured. "It'll be cleaned up by tonight."

"It better be."

"It will."

Shyly, I looked at them. "I—I mean—I can help," I said.

"Oh, no, Faye, that's fine," Mrs. Anderson said, and took one more look around her kitchen, then chuckled. "I'm going to expect a good treat out of this, girls. What are you making?"

"Brownies," Ellie said in a small voice.

"Well…look forward to eating them, I guess." She left.

I looked at Ellie sheepishly. "Sorry, Ellie."

But she brushed it off. "What is there to be sorry for? I started it."

"Well, I egged you on."

"Stop it, Faye." Ellie playfully shoved me. I shoved her back. "Should we start cleaning up now?"

"It's fine, we'll just mess it up again anyway since we're still baking. Besides, you're my best friend. I won't let you clean up such a disaster. I'll do it after you leave."

"What!?" I said. "And you're *my* best friend, Ell! No way am I letting you clean it up."

"My house," challenged Ellie.

"My mess," I responded.

"*Half* your mess," Ellie corrected.

We glared at each other for a few minutes, then I said, "Compromise?"

"How?"

"I clean up all the other baking stuff and you get the flour?"

Ellie considered. I could tell she wanted to get away with not letting me do anything, but she also knew me well enough to know I would never let her. "Fine."

"Great." I pulled the recipe book toward us. "Now let's get these brownies finished up."

•   •   •   •

An hour later, the brownies were finally in the oven and we were onto the job of cleaning.

"Did you know that when I was younger, Mom and I used to bake all the time?" I told Ellie as I placed the last bowl in the dishwasher.

"Really?" Ellie asked, wetting her fourth washcloth.

"Yeah," I said, smiling at the memory.

"How old were you? I never, ever remember you talking about it," said Ellie.

"I don't know," I said. "Four? Five? Six? One of those." I thought back to the good old days with a smile. Every week, I remembered, Mom would choose some sweet treat, and we'd bake it together, just the two of us. We'd make anything: cake, brownies, cupcakes, cookies...I loved rolling out the dough and cutting the fun shapes. But the all-time favorite of ours was the gingerdoodle. My mom had originally made it for the holidays one year, and I had loved it so much it had started to become a constant occasion. My mouth watered even now, remembering the sweet, crunchy combination of gingerbread and snickerdoodle that we made at least once a month, if not more.

"I wish we still did it," I said to nobody in particular.

"Why did you stop?" asked Ellie.

"I don't know, exactly." I shrugged. "Probably just got too hard, once Stella was born and stuff. And then maybe just too much time passed, and we forgot about it. Goodness, I never even thought of it until now."

"You didn't remember it until now?" Ellie leaned close, of course suddenly interested.

I groaned. "No, Ellie, I never *thought* of it until now. Not remember. I've always known we did it…" I trailed off, not sure if I was lying or not. Had I only dreamt it, maybe, or imagined it? The memory was hazy, but it was true. "No," I said firmly. "Ellie, this isn't just—I don't know—a dream or whatever. My mom and I really *did* do this."

Ellie shrugged nonchalantly. "Sure, whatever you say. How long are they in the oven for again?"

I checked the recipe and told Ellie, but my thoughts were elsewhere.

chapter fourteen

fantasy cookie

"Mom, remember when we used to bake all the time together?" I said confidently that night, after dinner. We had just finished cleaning up. Jack, who was currently grounded from his little "act" the previous night, was up in his room most likely plotting something sinister; Stella was out back playing with the neighbor girls, and Dad was sketching in his office, so it was just me and Mom. When Mom didn't answer right away, I went on. "Like, the gingerdoodle?"

Mom looked up from her book and laughed. "The *what*?"

I felt doubt for a moment, and then it dispersed. I knew this had happened; I *remembered* it.

Still, my voice was quiet. "Remember, Mom? The...the gingerdoodles? They were like a combination of gingerbread and…" I trailed off at Mom's look. "Sure, sweetie." Her gaze returned to her book.

"No, Mom, I'm serious. This isn't my imagination or whatever," I pressed. "We did bake," I echoed.

"Honey, sure we baked, but it wasn't like an everyday thing," she said. "We made cookies and stuff, but I *can* tell you I can't remember a single time making apparent 'gingerdoodly' or whatever."

"But…but…"

"Sweetie, I don't remember, as long as you've been here, baking anything in relation to a gingerdoodle." She laughed. "I would have remembered that name."

"But we *did*," I tried, suddenly feeling faint. "I *remember*."

"Well, if you say so," Mom said in a disregarding sort of way, and then went back to reading. "Why don't you go call Ellie or something? It's a beautiful night."

"I…" I sighed in relenting. "She's not home tonight."

I turned to go to my bedroom, and I traced the scar along my cheek. I suddenly remembered Brittney, telling me how her sister Heather had been killed. Amazement washed over me as I realized how truly lucky I had been to survive such an accident.

•   •   •   •

"What do you mean, your mom doesn't remember?" Ellie breathed the next afternoon.

We were outside, swinging on my swing set for lack of anything better to do, and I, mistakenly, had told her about the ordeal with the gingerdoodle and my mom's sudden absence of memory.

"You said it," I said miserably. "Ell, here's the thing. I remember this. I mean, the memory's vague, but it's there. It isn't just a dream. I *remember* it."

"And your mom doesn't?"

"Well, she says she does, but I think she's…like, not lying, but maybe just saying it to make me happy."

Silence. She pumped herself higher as she thought. "Well, haven't you been saying yourself how she's so edgy because of her pregnancy? What if the pregnancy also made her forgetful, the same way it's making her testy?"

"I—I don't know," I stammered, never even thinking of that possibility. "I guess—I mean—I never thought being pregnant made you forget things."

"There's a lot we don't know, Faye," offered Ellie. "For example, why is my hair red and yours brown?"

I laughed nervously.

"And why are the clouds white? Don't you think pink clouds would be pretty snazzy?"

"You're sidetracking, Ell," I said. "Just please help me figure this out. I really don't think I dreamed it. Do you think it's really just that Mom forgot?"

"I say it's plenty possible," Ellie declared. "Ask her if she remembers what she did on January second the year she was ten. She won't remember. People forget things."

"Ellie, *I* don't remember what I was doing that day the year I was *twelve*. And that's this past year. But Ellie, it just…She was just so 'whatever' about the whole thing."

The back door creaked before Ellie could answer, and Stella jumped out. "Faye, Mom says to come in for dinner."

"Okay," I said reluctantly, and jumped off the swing.

"Aw," Ellie said disappointingly. "Well, better off anyway, it's probably time for my dinner, too."

"Okay, bye then." I started towards the door; Ellie was still slowing her swing down.

"We're having chicken nuggets," Ellie said.

"Goodbye, Ellie."

"And French fries."

"See you later." I shut the door before she could stall any longer, but then stood there and watched her get off the swing, retrieve her flip-flops she had kicked off, and start walking back. When she saw me watching her, she waved emphatically, a huge grin on her face. I smiled back and waved back before heading into the kitchen to eat.

chapter fifteen
convincing dreams

Now that it was July, it was time to start counting down to my birthday.

The whole accident-crash thing, about me being in an car accident, freaked me out more than I had first anticipated; my nightmares returned, creepier and scarier than ever, mostly because now, I could connect them to the accident. I supposed my subconscious hadn't forgotten, while the rest of me had.

At first, I chose not to tell Ellie; combined with the whole apparent-false gingerdoodle memory, I wanted to have time to process on my own and didn't want the over-drama that came with telling my friend. I was just glad she hadn't overreacted about the gingerdoodle thing. It was too much for me to think about, so instead I dwelled upon the fact my birthday was fast approaching.

July twenty-third. July twenty-third. July twenty-third. I would be thirteen. It couldn't come soon enough.

Ellie was so excited, one would've guessed it was *her* birthday, not mine. Twelve days prior, she made up a song about it.

"Faye's b-day is in twelve days! It's gonna be-a craze! Faye's gonna be thirteen! I'd say I'm older but that'd be mean!" she sang one afternoon. We were at the park, the same one we'd met at so many years back. While Stella clambered on the monkey bars and tried to climb up the slide, we swung on the swings and talked.

"Ellie, that barely even rhymes," I said, laughing.

"It's creative *art*, Faye," she responded, and then leapt off the swing onto the mulch. "Aw, I almost beat my record."

While I found simply swinging enough, Ellie thought it was more fun to see how far she could jump from her swing. I watched with mild interest and much worry.

"What *I* want to know, Ellie," I said as she remounted her swing, "is why you make up a song for *my* birthday, rather than yours."

"Because you're my best friend, duh!" Ellie cried, kicking her legs to mount herself higher.

"Ellie," I sighed, and watched her for a minute. She began singing again as she swung higher and higher, and right as she finished she yelled,

"*MARSHIBILISN!*" and leapt off the swing.

I watched in amusement. "*What?*"

"What, what?"

"What in the whole world did you just yell?"

"Oh, that? It's a phrase from a book I read once." Ellie got up and dusted herself off, shrugging. "It just sounds cool, you know?"

"Whatever, Ell."

Ellie got back on the swing and started her routine again, which I soon learned went like this: sing Faye's birthday song, yell a random, strange word, jump off the swing. Repeat.

As this continued, the crash entered my brain, and despite my efforts to forget about it, it wouldn't leave. Finally I relented. Waiting for the moment when she was remounting, I said, "Ellie, let's talk."

"We *are* talking."

"No…" I sighed, and then before I could reconsider, I turned and blurted, "Ellie, did you know that when I was little I was in a car accident?"

"What?" Ellie's eyes popped and she fell off the swing. Alarmed, I stopped my own. "Are you okay?"

"What?" she repeated.

"My mom told me a week or so ago," I said. "It was the answer to the birthmark."

"Birth what?" Ellie sputtered, grabbing my swing handle and stopping me. "And why haven't I known?"

"Ellie, *I* didn't even know until recently. And you know, that mark on my cheek in the old photos we found?"

"Oh, that!" said Ellie. "So that's how you got it?" She leaned close.

"No, Ellie. Stella asked at dinner. Mom said that I was in a bad car accident when I was five, and then, when I was at the hospital, they had to do so much stuff on me they decided to remove the birthmark while they were at it."

"Ah," said Ellie. "Did I know you then?"

"Don't think so. I was five."

"That's horrid, Faye." Ellie shook her head somberly. "Why didn't your mom tell you before? And why don't you remember it?"

I shrugged. "I was real little, I guess."

"Not *that* little. You remembered the gingerdoodle thing, and wasn't that when you were younger than that? Besides, a wreck would be a big event. You couldn't just forget about it the way you could forget a…I don't know…an old dress or a friend's party."

"Huh." I'd never really thought of it that way, but she had a good point. "I'll ask my mom about it. Speaking of home, how long you wanna stay here?"

We were on our own for the afternoon; the only request from my father was that we take Stel. I felt kind of guilty; Mom, who was out for the afternoon, would never have let me go to the park on my own.

"I don't know," Ellie said. "Maybe ten more minutes or something. I mean, look at all the fun Stel's having."

I followed her gaze and almost choked. Stella was now sitting atop the monkey bars, kicking her legs back and forth and looking very proud of herself.

"So," Ellie said brightly, "What's the Brittster been up to lately?"

I shrugged. "Same old, same old. She just does her work and then leaves."

"You should talk to her, Faye. People need company when they're working."

"I don't know, Ell, I've just been so busy." I didn't want to tell Ellie that that wasn't all. These days I had a weird feeling about Brittney, and felt uncomfortable around her. It felt like she was hiding something specifically from me and it bothered me, made me feel strange.

"Busy? Some excuse," she said.

"No, really, Ellie. My birthday's coming up in a week or so. I've been too preoccupied to worry about Brittney."

"Worry?"

"Okay, too preoccupied to *think* about Brittney. Think, worry, what's the difference?"

"What does *preoccupied* even mean?"

"It means, like—never mind! Elisabeth Anderson, you know what it means."

Ellie scowled and gave me a shove. "I don't like when you call me that."

"I don't like when you mess around with me like that," I countered, crossing my own arms.

A stare-down was engaged, one in which I

won.

"Fine. I won't mess with you if you don't call me Elisabeth."

I laughed. "Deal."

Ellie jumped back on her swing. "Now back to that challenge."

"What challenge?" I asked.

"How far I can jump!" she said. "What, do you have *amneeesia* or something?" Suddenly her eyes grew large. "That's it, Faye! I've figured out the mystery. You have amnesia!"

"Ellie," I groaned, but she persisted. "Faye, seriously. I mean it."

"Ellie!" I sighed, and checked my watch.

"Seriously, Ellie," I said, then got off my swing. "Let's go back. My dad's probably expecting us by now, anyway."

•　　•　　•　　•

My birthday drew closer and closer. I wasn't going to have a party, but Mom did say I could go someplace of my choice with Ellie. I chose the local neighborhood pool—having a birthday at the end of July meant I normally got hot, hot weather, great for swimming. Ellie thought I was crazy and that I should have chosen the huge waterpark, but I wanted a quieter place to just have fun and not worry about staying near Mom or anything.

I wanted to invite Logan, too. When I asked Mom, she frowned. "Logan?" asked Mom. "You haven't seen him all summer, Faye."

"Just because there's no school. And all the more reason to invite him," I said, and so Mom reluctantly agreed. Using Mom's phone—when would I ever get my own?—I sent him a quick text.

FAYE: hey logan. it's faye. my bdays the 23rd of next week. wanted to invite u to my small party. We're going to swim at neighborhood pool (riverside) at 3:30. just me, u, & ellie. then having pizza & stuff at my house. see u there?
LOGAN: sweet! sounds gr8. i'm there! happy early bday!
FAYE: why thx u logan :)
LOGAN: how r u txting me? i thought u didnt have a phone.
FAYE: my moms phone. my ipod broke remember
LOGAN: lol didn't ell break it
FAYE: no it fell out of case and shattered
LOGAN: shame
FAYE: gtg talk to u later
LOGAN: u mean ttyl
FAYE: whatever c u soon
LOGAN: see u!!

I sighed loudly and placed the phone in Mom's outstretched hand.

"Mom, don't you think it's high time I have my own iPod again?"

Last year, I'd gotten a brand-new, nice iPod touch for my birthday. Two months later, it had slipped out of its carrying case and shattered on the cement below. I had tried to get it working again, but nothing worked, so ever since, I'd had to rely on Mom to talk to friends.

"Well, your birthday's coming up. You never know," Mom said, but I couldn't tell if that meant legitimately "maybe," or if it meant, "I've already gotten it for you."

I sighed.

•　　•　　•　　•

"Wake up, birthday girl!" Mom says in my ear. I open my eyes and roll over, grinning at her. It's Mom, but her hair is brown again, her eyes dark. She's grinning, too. "Your birthday breakfast is waiting downstairs, honey. And your sibs are dying to give you presents!" I laugh, and get out of bed. The floor is cold, so cold that I stuff my feet into socks. Downstairs, Mom puts a pancake on my plate, and I stuff it down. "Snow!" someone yells, and I rush to the back door, press my hands against it. It's cold, so cold, beneath my fingers. Outside, the world is white, snow fluttering down to rest on the ground. "I'm going to play outside!" I loudly declare. And I do: slipping on new pink snow boots and a new pink hat, I race outside into the snowy wonder. The snowflakes float down on me, soft and delicate, gentle and kind as I laugh and giggle in the snow.

*The air is cold, but I don't mind. I bend down to roll a
snowball, but as I roll it, my foot somehow slips and I fall,
face-first, into pavement. I look up to find myself suddenly
back in the car crash, aware of screaming. I hear glass shatter
and look to my right through the broken window to see the
snow, still so graceful, yet floating down on top of everything,
coating everything in white.*

My eyes opened to see the white ceiling. I laid in
bed, unmoving, wondering if I was still dreaming,
marveling over the bizarreness.

I had dreamed about the accident, and it had
turned out to be true. Suddenly I felt fearful. What
if all the things I dreamed had happened to me
really had happened?

I closed my eyes tightly, bringing back the
dream. *Snow*, someone had said. *Snow* on my
birthday. But my birthday was in July. How could
there be snow?

A memory—or dream?—flooded back to me.
Somebody—I couldn't get the face—giving me
snow boots for my birthday. My joy, my happiness.
Running outside in my new boots, eager to try them
out.

When had that been? When had it happened?
Had it only been a dream?

I slung myself out of bed, making up my mind,
for the moment, to forget about it.

Downstairs, Mom had breakfast ready for me,

not unlike in the dream. Except in this case, "having breakfast ready" meant she had taken the effort to get a box of cereal out and put it on the counter. Mom herself was nowhere to be found and the cereal was the one I didn't like.

After finishing a very silent and lonely breakfast, I went to find the rest of the family. I found Mom outside on the front porch. Her sketchpad was beside her, but it lay untouched. She rocked back and forth on the bench swing, gazing out on the beautiful landscape, of the sun shining down on the peaceful neighborhood.

"Mom?" I said, and she looked up at my voice. "Faye! How nice it is to see you! How are you doing?"

"Good. How are you? Why are you out here?"

"Oh…not much…" Mom seemed distraught. "The doctor said fresh air might be good, that I should try to get some more." She smiled thinly. "The baby wants to come."

"What?" Suddenly I was alarmed. "But my birthday's coming up next week!"

Mom began to laugh. "Not that soon, Faye. But I think it'll be sooner than we think."

I nodded, sitting next to her on the bench, and we swung back and forth, watching the neighborhood around us. The brick two-story houses were beautiful, complete with high roofs, three-car garages and neatly trimmed lawns. The landscapes were gorgeous; across the street, Mrs. Fambrough's flowers were a pleasure to look at, their radiant colors reflecting off the sunlight. A few joggers ran by, and down the street, a few little kids were riding their bikes. The sky was clear, the sun was shining, and combined with the pretty sounds of birds twittering, it seemed like a perfect morning. It wasn't normal that I was up this early outside of school and only now was I beginning to see the beauty in it.

A little while later the screen door slammed and then Stella was there. "What are you doing?" she demanded.

I laughed at her tone. "Just sitting out here, Stel. Isn't it such a beautiful morning?"

Stella looked around. "Yeah, I guess. Can I sit with you on the bench?"

"Sure," I said, shrugging and moving over. My little sister slid in beside me and rested her head on my shoulder. "I had a bad dream last night," she announced.

"I'm sorry, Stel," I said, knowing all too well what that felt like. "Do you want to tell us?"

"Tell us what?" Intruder Jack interrupted our conversation by coming onto the porch. He let the screen door slam behind him and then tapped his iPod screen to turn off the music in his headphones—or maybe turn it on, who knew. "Can I be apart of this, or is it girl talk?" he added sarcastically.

"No, do join us, Jack," Mom said welcomingly. Seeing no place to sit, my big brother sat down on the porch floor, sitting up against the porch railing and returning his gaze to his iPod.

"So," Jack said, his eyes on his screen, "what were you gonna say, Stella-Stellie?"

Stella ignored the name. "None of your business," she said snootily.

"Stella had a bad dream," Mom said. "But she doesn't have to share if she doesn't want to."

"Which I don't," Stella said indignantly.

"Bad dreams, huh?" Jack said. "Well, if anyone cares, I have dreams, too." He shivered. "I had a pretty creepy one last night."

"Are you going to tell us?" Stella asked.

Jack scoffed. "Course not," he said.

"Jack," Mom said warningly.

Jack shook his head lightly. Then, tapping his iPod screen, he got up and opened the screen door to go back inside, but then stopped, catching me watching him. We locked gazes for an instant, and he said vaguely, "I dreamed you went away...and you never came back."

I didn't have time to puzzle over these strange words before the door slammed behind him.

"Well, that was a short visit," Mom commented as Stella shifted positions to try to get on Mom's lap. Laughing, Mom gently pushed her off. "I'm a pregnant woman, silly. I can't hold you on my lap."

Stella pouted, but she obliged, sitting down on next to Mom on the other side of the swing.

"Mom?" I said, carefully choosing my words.

"What, sweetie?"

"Did I—I mean—did we—did we ever go somewhere for my birthday when I was younger?" As I finished, I suddenly felt embarrassed at how strange the question had sounded.

"Go somewhere?" Mom lifted her eyebrows. "Well, probably—"

"No." I interrupted her. "Not like to the ice cream place or anything. Like…another state. Or something."

Mom seemed alarmed, I didn't know why. "What, honey? Why do you ask?"

"I don't know. I…thought I remembered a birthday where I…this sounds crazy…where it was snowing?"

"Snowing?" Stella said in disbelief. "Your birthday's in *July*, Faye! How could it be snowing?"

"I know," I said grumpily. "That's why I asked. Maybe we went somewhere where it was snowing?"

Mom was frowning. "I don't recall anything of the sort, sweetie. You probably just had a convincing dream."

I frowned, too. "Great. So now I'm a crazy person who mistakes their dreams for reality?"

"No, no, no," Mom laughed. "Not at all. It happens to everyone. I've had dreams at first I thought was real."

"But it's been a while since I woke. Shouldn't it have worn off by now? I mean, I still feel like I can remember it." I didn't mention the memory of getting snow boots I had recalled after I had awoken.

"Some dreams certainly can be like that, honey," Mom assured me. She reached down and picked up the sketchpad she'd laid on the porch floor when Stella and me had decided to come sit by her. Now she took it back, along with the pencil, and ran it along the perimeter of the paper. Leaning into Stel, she said, "So, Stella-girl, what do you think of this one? I'm trying a new idea…"

I grumbled and got up, leaning against the porch railing; I didn't understand the joy of house designing the way Stella did. I mean, all I saw it as was different size squares. Of course I saw the importance in it—it would, in turn, probably turn into some house someday—but I didn't particularly enjoy watching Mom draw.

Outside, the grass was wet with dew, and the sky was a beautiful blue. Already, I could feel the humidity of what was sure to be a hot day. Which made me question again about the snow. There was no way that snow was possible on a day this time of year.

So why was the image so fresh, so real in my mind?

chapter sixteen

a start to a great year

As days flew by, the thought faded, though it was always there, in the back of my mind, a mystery begging to be unraveled. At the same time, I kept telling myself that there was nothing to be unraveled; it had all been a dream.

July 22nd, I woke up and was faced with the bright reality that there was only one more day to wait. One more day of being twelve. Tomorrow, the world of being a teenager opened up to me. Not that I didn't enjoy being twelve; it was just that I was looking forward to being thirteen. Ellie, who'd turned thirteen five months earlier, didn't help my anticipation with her constant teasing of how much fun being thirteen was.

The morning dragged by. By 11 o'clock, I was dying of boredom and so I got Mom's permission to call up Ellie and invite her over. It was Monday, and Brittney was coming as well. I knew that Ellie would turn the afternoon into some big kind of mystery or adventure, and even though sometimes Ellie's ideas annoyed me, it was just what I needed to pass the time today.

After checking with her mom to make sure she was available, Ellie promised to be at my house at 12:30. I had originally told her one, but she wouldn't hear of it once she heard Brittney was coming. "Twelve," she'd insisted. "We need time to plan."

"Plan?"

"Work with me, Faye. I'll be there at twelve."

"I'm eating lunch then, Ell, my mom will not like that."

She grumbled, but compromised. "Twelve-thirty, then."

Now, as I hung up the phone, a thought occurred to me that this was the last time I would hang out with Ellie as a twelve-year-old. Even though it seemed silly, it still shot a thrill through me.

At exactly 12:31, the doorbell rang. I got up to answer it, not before it'd rang twice more.

"Britt's not here, is she?" Ellie asked as she entered, taking a quick survey of the downstairs.

"Not yet, she's not. Do you see a car in the driveway?" I led her into the kitchen area, where Stella was eating chocolate chip cookies that she'd insisted on baking that morning. She'd offered to let me "help" (even though it was more likely the other way around) and even Mom had taken her side, saying what a good time-passer it was. But I hadn't wanted to; the last time I baked, it had stirred unwanted—*memories?*—*dreams?*

Now, I helped myself to one of the many cookies sitting on the plate on the counter and sunk my teeth in. "Delish, Stel."

She scowled at me instead of thanking me, and watched Ellie take one, too. After taking a bite, Ellie closed her eyes, put her hand on her stomach, and uttered a contended, happy, extremely loud groan of satisfaction.

"Man," she said, opening her eyes and focusing on my sister's face, "these are absolutely, positively, without a doubt, the most delicious cookies I have ever seen or eaten in my whole entire thirteen years of life."

Stella just stared at her. "What?"

"You made them for Britt, didn't ya?" said Ellie, stuffing the rest of the cookie in her mouth and making a grab for a second.

"What? *Ellie*," I said, but Stella had other ideas. "Of course I did," she said, and huffed with annoyance even though I knew the idea had only entered her mind a minute ago when Ellie had suggested it.

Ellie was halfway through her second. "Oh my goodness, Stel, this is just perfect bliss. Never has so fine a cookie entered my mouth. Britt will love them."

"Whoa there!" I said. "Who says we're giving the cleaning lady our cookies? And why the drama?"

Ellie shrugged. "Just in the mood, I guess."

Stella's face crumpled. "You *don't* like my cookies?"

I sighed. "Let's get out of here." I grabbed Ellie's sleeve, turned to go—and found myself face-to-face with my mother.

"Faye, stop being so mean to your sister," she said. "What's going on here? Why is it so wrong to offer Brittney cookies? It sounds pretty nice to me."

"I—I don't know." Now that I thought about it, I didn't know why I ever had a problem with it. "I just—thought—that they were for the family?"

"Giving one to Brittney isn't a loss on our part, Faye. Actually, considering the work she's doing, it would be a nice bonus."

"Yeah…" I felt uncomfortable under her gaze suddenly, and it alarmed me. I shouldn't feel uncomfortable around my own mother. Feeling strange about Brittney…well, she was the cleaning lady, and only here a few times a week….

Mom shook her head, shaking me from my thoughts. "Just leave Stel alone, Faye." Noticing Ellie, she said, "Hello, Ellie," before heading past us into the kitchen.

We'd be better off to leave Stella alone, anyway. I brought Ellie upstairs to my room, but as soon as we arrived, she glimpsed the time—12:55—on my clock and insisted we return downstairs so we'd be there to "see Britt's entrance."

Turned out "Britt" was early, so by the time we got downstairs Mom was letting her in. "Aw, man!" said Ellie under her breath.

Brittney smiled warmly at us. "Hello, girls. How are you doing?"

"Fine," I said.

"Extravagant!" Ellie, as always, chose to be overdramatic. "And guess what's tomorrow."

"July 23rd?" Brittney guessed good-naturedly. "Tuesday?"

"Nope," Ellie said with satisfaction, then realized exactly what Brittney had guessed. "Oh— well, it is those things, but it's something else too."

"I give up. What?"

"*Faye's birthday!*" Ellie announced proudly, excitedly, while I rolled my eyes beside her. I could have seen this coming.

"Really?" Brittney looked me up and down. "Well, a very happy birthday to you…Faye!"

"Thanks," I said, blushing.

"How old will you be?" she asked, carefully. "Thirteen."

"Right." She smiled. "Thirteen's a lot of fun. Have a great day. Doing anything special?"

As she said this, she made her way through the house, dragging her bucket of supplies behind her.

"Yeah, I'm going to the pool with Ellie and my friend, Logan."

"Logan, right. You've told me about him before," Brittney said. "Well, that's cool. I hope you have fun."

Stella came running up to us. "Brittney! I made cookies. Do you want to try them?" she panted. Gone was the annoyed, scowling little girl I'd seen earlier, replaced by a more cheerful, sweet version of my sister.

"Cookies? I never resist those." Brittney left us to follow Stel into the kitchen, where the plate of cookies laid waiting.

I sighed. "Let's go upstairs, Ell."

"Are you kidding? I want to talk with the Britt some more." Ellie abandoned me and walked over to where Brittney was eating one of Stella's cookies, while Stella stood beside and beamed with pride. Reluctantly I followed her over, in time to hear Brittney comment on how delicious they were.

"So, Britt." Ellie leaned on her elbows on the counter.

Brittney looked up, alarmed. "Don't call me that, please. Brittney suits me fine."

"Whatever." Ellie shrugged, and I winced inwardly, wishing she could be more polite. It wasn't that Ellie was rude, not directly; it was just that she got so caught up in her funny comments, phrases, and jokes that she forgot, sometimes, that some occasions required more thoughtfulness toward others. "So, how's your life going?"

Brittney raised her eyebrows. "It's going fine."

"So is mine, what a coincidence."

Brittney gave a small smile at that, but then she wiped her hands off on a napkin and looked at us. "Well, I'm gonna get to work. Where'd your mother go?"

"I'm in here, Brittney," Mom called from the front. "You can just go ahead with your Monday routine. If you have any questions, don't hesitate."

"Thank you, Mrs. Corcoran." Brittney smiled at us, and headed upstairs. Mondays were carpet-cleaning days.

Ellie tried to persuade me into following Brittney, but I protested that she didn't want two kids stalking her while she cleaned. We went to find Mom and she asked us to get the mail for her. Since Ellie and I were too lazy to put on shoes, we tromped outside barefoot to the mailbox.

Seeing all the letters there reminded me of my would-be pen pal Naomi, but Jack had so ruthlessly destroyed my only chance at keeping in touch with her. I felt a pang of sadness; I would have so loved to keep in touch with her.

"What's up, Faye?"

I explained about Naomi.

She looked at me sadly. "I'm sorry, friend."

"Friend?" I arched my eyebrows. "Since when do you call me—"

"Know what's funny?" she interrupted. "When we first met, you always used to call me Naomi."

"What?" I exclaimed, looking at her funny.

"Yeah," she said. "I'd always have to correct you. We thought it was so funny. I mean, my name doesn't sound *anything* like Naomi, yet you always called me it."

"Huh," I said, frowning. "That is funny. Oh well. Come on, let's go back inside and see what there is to do."

•　　•　　•　　•

Like I'd planned, the day flew by. Before I knew it, I was going to bed. Lying there fidgeting, I wondered how in the world I could sleep. I stared at the digital clock at my bedside: 9:23. 9:24. 9:25. In under three hours, the clock would strike midnight. I would no longer be twelve. I would be thirteen, an official teenager, and it would be my birthday.

I decided to try to stay up until midnight, but my body had other plans. By ten, I couldn't keep my eyes open. I found myself drifting into sleep, drifting into a dream.

"Let's go get ice cream, honey!" Mom says cheerfully, getting me into the car, but once again, it's brown-haired Mom. "There's no better way to celebrate a little girl's birthday, especially if it's such a special girl as you." She helps me buckle my seat; I'm young, still being strapped into the baby seat. Next to me, Ellie sits, but an older version of her, her thirteen-year-old self. She's Ellie, but she looks different: deep brown hair, and no glasses. I'm about to ask where they are when suddenly Mom slams on the brakes. I didn't even realize the car had started, but suddenly I am thrust forward.

The belt around me snaps, and I find myself on the floor of the car. I scream Ellie's name and look up to where she was sitting, but she isn't there. The window across from me is gone, the glass obliterated. I scream again, and then I hear a voice. I turn around and see Mom, this time looking just like her normal self, reaching towards me and speaking softly. "Everything's okay, honey. Just come with me. Come with me and you'll be fine."

My eyes popped open. My heart was thudding in my chest.

Outside was still dark. The silence was deafening.

I shook my head to rid myself of the dreams. Then I remembered.

A slow smile slid across my face.

It was my birthday. I was thirteen.

My dreams forgotten, I stared at the ceiling, excitement shooting through me. It was unusually quiet in the house, and I stole a glance at the clock. 8:30 a.m. Mom would be up, Dad would have already left for work, and Stella would be downstairs causing trouble while Jack slept until at least ten. Why was it so quiet?

I jumped out of bed. This was the first time getting up being thirteen. I walked downstairs slowly, enjoying each step.

At the sound of footsteps on the stairs, Mom looked up. "Look who's awake! Happy birthday, sweetie!"

"Thanks!" I went and hugged her, then looked

around. "Where's Stel?"

"*Surprise!*" Stella jumped out from behind the counter island and threw colored balloons in the air, grinning and laughing. "Surprise surprise double surprise and triple surprise! Happy birthday, Faye!"

"Stel!" I was aghast. Grinning, I bent to hug her. "That was *awesome*! Thank you!"

"Happy birthday," she said again, then crinkled her nose. "How old are you again?"

I laughed. "Do you really not know?"

"Fourteen?"

"Thirteen." I laughed, amused she didn't know and glad for the surprise she had gone out of her way to give me.

"Right. Ellie's thirteen already, right?"

"Yeah, she's like five months older than me."

"Right," Stella said, nodding slowly. "Claire's older than me, too, but only by a few months."

Stella's friends, in general, were very limited. At school, she had a few good friends, but she rarely saw them over the summer. Claire, along with her sisters, Abby and Gracie, lived down the street and were a good option for playtime during the summer, but when the school year came around, Stel didn't see them as they went to a private school. Stella didn't seem to mind, although she often complained how unfair it was that I had a friend like Ellie over all the time and she didn't.

"So, party tonight, right?" Stella giggled, dancing around. I nodded, full of anticipation and excitement. "You got that right!" I couldn't wait for my sure-to-be-amazing birthday bash that night. After a swim at the pool, we were going to come back to my house, where we'd have pizza and cake, open presents, and then play games outside in the dark. With Ellie living down the street and Logan living in the neighborhood as well, it wouldn't be a problem to stay outside late.

My dream birthday involved no chores, but since I had chosen to do my party actually on my birthday, that idea was out the window. As soon as I was dressed, Mom put me to work. Brittney had done the hard, dirty work, but there were still the basic chores to do. First, my room. "You have guests coming; it needs to be clean," Mom had told me. Then picking up around the house. Kitchen chores came last after lunch and after I'd finished baking my cake. I'd wanted Ellie to come help me, but Mom told me that it was impolite since there was only one other guest coming, so I did it on my own.

After a much-too-long wait, it was finally time to get into our swimsuits, get our swimming stuff, and leave to pick up Ellie and Logan.

I slipped on my swimsuit and grabbed the two pool noodles from the basement, followed by getting my goggles. Mom tucked her iPhone into the bag at my protest. I wanted every minute of this captured through either picture or video.

Dad had taken a half-day at work, and was back by one o'clock so he could come, too.

At 3:20, we assembled in the car. I sat in the

back by the two empty seats for Ellie and Logan; Jack and Stella sat ahead of me, and Mom and Dad were in the front. I shook with excitement as I did a quick check that I had everything: goggles, pool noodles, towels...

First stop was Ellie's. She ran out the second the car pulled in the drive, yelling an emphatic "Bye!" to her mom as she ran. I leaned over and pushed the button for the automatic door, and she clambered in, grinning. "I'm so excited! This is going to be a blast! Oh, and happy birthday! Here's your gift." She thrust a gift bag, stuffed with multicolored wrapping paper, at me.

"Thanks," I said, grinning, and then turned around and put it in the trunk, like Mom had told me prior.

"I'll open it at home, after cake," I explained to Ellie.

Logan's house was a couple of streets over. He wasn't waiting on the porch like Ellie had been, so Ellie and me had the pleasure of going up and getting him. As we mounted the steps, Ellie was struck with sudden inspiration. "Let's ding-dong-ditch him!"

I laughed. "What?"

"No, really. It'll be funny. Come on!" Ellie dragged me up to the door, both of us laughing. I wouldn't do such a radical thing on my own, but it *was* my birthday. I rolled my eyes and went along with it.

Ellie pressed the doorbell and dragged me to

the end of the porch and crouched down, both of us giggling like crazy. Mom rolled down her window and called, "What are you doing? We have to get going."

"We're ding-dong-ditching. It won't take long," Ellie called back, laughing.

Dad laid a hand on Mom's arm. "It's her birthday, Kim."

The door creaked open, and Logan stepped out. "Faye? Ellie?" He turned and saw us. "Ha, ha, very funny. Come on, let's go!"

Disappointed our prank hadn't worked to its full extent, but still full of excitement and giggles nevertheless, we clambered in the car after Logan. Mom smiled in the rear view mirror. "How are you, Logan?"

"Just fine, Mrs. Corcoran. Thanks for including me," he said politely.

"Of course. Faye's birthday wouldn't be complete without both her friends," Mom said, smiling.

Logan turned and brushed his hair out of his eyes. "Excited, Faye?"

"More than it," I laughed. "I'm so glad you both can come."

"You're *glad*?" Ellie laughed. "And we're stoked!"

Logan nodded in agreement, then grinned mischievously. "Okay. I challenge both of you to a race when we get there. Across the whole pool. Unless you already have something planned, Faye?"

"No, we can just have fun," I said.

Ellie scowled at him. "Oh, Logo, you know I'm a slowpoke at swimming!" Ellie laughed, but she didn't refuse the challenge.

It was a nice, hot day, but the pool wasn't too crowded. The pool had one slide that twisted once before dumping us into the water. We headed there first. Stella trailed behind, trying to keep up, and for once, I wasn't annoyed. I did wonder where Jack was, but didn't give it much thought. As long as he wasn't stalking me or trying to prank me, I didn't care much where he was.

At the slide, the lifeguard next to it motioned for us to go, one at a time. Ellie and Logan insisted I go first, and I slid into the pool, feeling joyful. It was my birthday: a start of another great year. The time at the pool went by way too fast. Before we knew it, it was time to head back. And even after a million races and a zillion water games, I wasn't ready to leave. Out of the water, the air was cold on me. It reminded me of my strange dream of snow, and with a sudden urge, turned to Ellie.

"Ellie," I said, "know what's strange?"

"Strange?" Ellie was immediately interested. "What's strange?"

"I remember snow on my birthday," I said. "I mean, I remember like, celebrating in snow."

Nearby, Mom had stopped packing things up and stood, listening. I felt uncomfortable for a minute, and then shrugged it off. She was my mom, after all. She had the right to want to know what I was saying to Ellie, and it wasn't like I was whispering in private.

"Snow? On your birthday? What, were you visiting Alaska?" said Ellie, raising her eyebrows and pulling her towel closer around her.

"I don't know. I mean, no. I mean, maybe. I don't remember details."

"Did you just remember this?"

"Yes—I mean, I think so. I had a dream about it."

"So it's a dream?"

"No, I think I remember it more as a memory." Ellie studied me. Then she said, "We'll talk later."

Logan surfaced near us, swam over, and lifted himself out of the pool, shivering. "Aw, Faye, isn't it your birthday? Can't you request we stay longer? Like two more hours?"

I laughed. "Don't you want cake and ice cream?"

"Ice cream?" Logan went over and got his towel. "That settles it. We're going. I'm starving."

"You're starving?" said Ellie. "Well, it doesn't matter how hungry you are. I'm so famished I could eat this towel." She shook it in his face.

"I'd like to see you do it," said Logan.

"Nah, not hungry enough." Ellie nonchalantly folded her towel and tucked it in her bag while I stifled laughter.

We piled into the car. First we were going to pick up the pizza, then go back home. As we drove,

Ellie's hunger turned into something beyond hunger.

It started with a brown mailbox on the side of the road. "That looks like a chocolate brownie," she said, pointing it out. "I'm so hungry I'm seeing things. Great."

"*What* looks like a brownie?" Logan laughed, leaning over.

"Hey! That looks like green M&Ms!" Ellie cried, pointing emphatically at an upcoming stoplight. Logan laughed out loud. I put my head in my hands.

"You okay back there, Ellie?" Mom called.

"She's fine," Logan laughed.

"No, I'm not," Ellie said, and then thoughtfully looked at her foot. "Shoes rather remind me of cake pops," she commented, throwing us into further laughter.

Upon stopping at the pizza place to pick up pizza, Ellie started raving on how good the smell was and how she was going to faint if she didn't eat soon.

"That looks like pizza!" she said suddenly, thrusting her finger up ahead. I followed her gaze to see Dad coming back to the car, carrying two pizzas. I laughed and groaned at the same time. "Ellie Anderson!"

When we got home we stumbled out of the car, hungry and wet, and went inside to change. Ellie, of course, had forgotten a change of clothes and so had to borrow some of mine instead.

Once we were finally all dressed, we sat around the table to eat. Logan rubbed his hands together. "Mmm! Pizza! I *love* pizza!"

"We're aware of that, Logo," said Ellie.

Logan scowled at her while taking a big bite. His scowl immediately disappeared. "Man, this is scrumptious," he said, his mouth full.

Ellie rolled her eyes while taking a bite of her own piece. Then her eyes widened. "Goodness, he's right!"

I took a bite of my own slice. "Mmm, it is good. Probably because we're all so hungry."

"Hungry? I could eat this whole pizza," Logan bragged.

"Really?" Ellie laughed. "I'd like to see you do it."

Logan ended up eating almost half. We got a good laugh out of it.

Mom lit the cake candles. I smiled, unable to contain my grin, as the song was started: "Happy birthday to you, happy birthday to you, happy birthday dear Faye, happy birthday to you!"

I took a breath and extinguished the thirteen candles in one breath. Ellie clapped dramatically and Logan cheered, "Go, go, Fayster!"

I laughed. "Since when do you call me that?"

"Yeah, Logester," Ellie said. "That's *my* nickname!"

After cake we opened presents. Ellie gave me a bunch of neon-colored duct tape, along with a book on making things with duct tape, and Logan gifted a new set of colored pens and a sketchbook. Stella excitedly presented her box. I opened it to find a new pair of sparkly earrings and a necklace. I lifted them up and smiled at my grinning sister. "Thanks, Stel!"

"It's from me and Jack," she said, "because Jack didn't want to go shopping."

I laughed.

Then Mom handed me a wrapped box with a twinkle in her eye and said, "Happy birthday, honey."

"Open it, open it!" sang Ellie.

Carefully I peeled back the wrapping paper— and let out a squeal, ripping off the rest of the paper. "An iPod touch? Really?"

"Faye!" screamed Ellie, jumping up and down with excitement. "You will *finally* be able to text!"

I felt like jumping myself and at the same time, laughing at Ellie's drama. "Mom, thank you, thank you, *thank you* so much!"

Stella pouted. "Mom, why does Faye get to have an iPod, but I don't?"

"Well, honey," Mom said, "Faye's older. When you turn thirteen, you'll be like Faye, too."

Stella didn't seem to take this as a good answer, but I wasn't paying attention anymore.

After an hour of me, Logan, and Ellie playing with my brand-new iPod, we decided to go outside. We each got a bunch of glow sticks and a flashlight, then ran outside, laughing and ready for some summer night fun.

The summer air was humid, but not overwhelmingly hot; the sky was clear and no sign of rain. Logan, Ellie, and I, along with Stella (who insisted on tagging along) had a blast running around, playing silly games, and laughing.

By the end of the night, two things were clear to me: one, I was worn out; and two, this was ultimately the best birthday I'd had so far.

chapter seventeen
my baby sibling

My birthday had been undoubtedly the best yet, and as well the next few days were bliss as well. I spent time lounging around the house, making duct tape things, drawing, and mostly messing around with my iPod, texting Logan and Ellie every time I found out something else about it.

But nothing compared to what happened a few days later. I had gone to bed late, around 10:30, and fell asleep quickly.

Then, sometime in the night, something woke me up.

Noise. Movement, outside my closed door. Voices, talking in low tones. I rolled over and looked at the clock: 2:01 a.m. *Who in the world was up at two in the morning?*

Curiosity overcame sleepiness. I stepped out

of my bed, shivering, and tiptoed to the door. I slid it open and blinked in the hall light. "What's going on?"

Jack rushed towards me from across the loft, grinning. "Faye, you're awake!"

"What's going on?" I repeated, rubbing my eyes.

"It's Mom!" he cried. "She's in labor!"

"What?" I was awake in a second. "So we're leaving? For the hospital? I have to get dressed!" I turned to go back to my room until Jack stopped me. "No, we're going to Ellie's. Dad's trying to get a hold of them now."

My heart sunk. "What?"

Dad appeared in the loft. "Great, Faye, you're up." His voice was urgent. "Okay, guys, get Stel up and let's go. Hurry!"

I raced back to my room to throw on clothes while Jack woke up Stella. Ellie or not, I wasn't leaving the house in pajamas. Five minutes later, we rushed downstairs, where Dad gathered the last few necessities. "Get in the car, kids. We'll be there in a minute."

I clambered into the car after my siblings; Jack sat in front and Stella and I slid into the middle seats to give Mom the whole backseat to herself. Still in pajamas, Stella giggled uncontrollably. "I'm gonna be a big sister!"

Though we were probably in the car two minutes before Mom and Dad arrived, it seemed like hours. Mom moaned as she finally slid into the backseat, and Dad hurriedly started the car.

Jack turned around in his seat. "You okay, Mom?"

"Fine." It sounded forced. I looked out the window, my heart-rate rapidly increasing by the moment. I was going to have a new sibling! Maybe even within hours!

The thought occurred to me suddenly that it was only July 30th, and the baby wasn't due until late August. It was nearly a month early. Alarmed, I looked at Dad, then Mom. "Dad! The baby's a month early! Will it be okay?"

"It'll be fine, Faye." Dad's voice sounded oddly forced as we drove through the quiet residental streets. Only when we had exited the neighborhood did I remember what Jack had said. "We're not going to Ellie's?"

"She won't pick up, and your mother can't wait any longer. We'll have them pick you up in the morning." The car sped along the streets, faster than it probably should have, but nobody complained. The ride was silent; I sat, watching the dark landscape speed by, hoping everything was going to be okay. Despite Dad's words, I couldn't shake the worry about the baby, and about Mom.

After 20 minutes, Dad smoothly exited the highway and swerved around a corner. Calling back to the backseat, he said, "Are you doing okay, Kimberly?"

"Just get us there soon."

Within minutes, we pulled into the emergency

room. The sky was dark, and the glowing, red lights seemed to stare at me as we helped Mom out of the car. The ER. We were at the ER. I desperately tried to assure myself everything would be fine, but would it?

Before I knew it, Jack, Stella and I had been escorted up to a waiting room in the Labor & Delivery Unit. Dad rushed through versions of "It'll be fine!" and "I'll check on you whenever I can," before hurrying off to the room where Mom was going to give birth to my new sibling.

"Whew!" Jack flopped down on a stiff, padded chair. I looked around the hospital, at the hallways of doors, at the waiting room full of chairs we sat in. Across the room, a nurse sat at a desk.

The whole thing—coming to the hospital, the hospital itself, the rush—seemed vaguely familiar, but I couldn't place why.

"Sudden," I said.

"What?" Jack asked.

"This whole thing. Sudden. And Jack, the baby's a whole month early. Do you think it'll be alright?"

"What makes you ask *me* that?" Jack leaned back in his chair and looked at the ceiling, his expression vague.

"Faye," Stella mumbled sleepily, curling up in a ball on a chair, "Is it okay to sleep in a waiting room?"

"Sure, Stel." In fact, I was considering it myself.

"Wake me up when the baby comes?"

"Of course." Provided I wasn't sleeping myself, of course.

Stella was asleep within minutes. Jack was still wide awake, tapping his foot impatiently, then getting up and pacing around the room before sitting down to resume tapping.

I watched him for a while, and found myself constantly growing sleepier. "Are you planning on sleeping?" I asked him.

He looked at me like I was crazy. "Are you kidding me? Of course not."

"Well, don't you have something better to do than just pace? Your iPod or something?"

"Forgot it in the craziness of this morning," he replied, and sat down and yawned. "Wow, was this really this morning?" Without waiting for an answer, he looked at me. "How about you? Do you have that brand-new electronic of yours?"

"Forgot it," I grumbled, and after a moment, curled up in the chair like my sister. "Wake me when the baby comes, okay?" It wasn't the most comfortable place to sleep, but I was tired, and besides, sleeping would pass the time.

Jack sighed. "Fine, but if you miss the *moment*, don't blame me. The baby will be here any minute, you know."

Despite the events of the night, I was suddenly very tired. I also knew that labor and birth wasn't a five-minute event and it would at least be a few hours before the baby arrived. I decided against correcting my brother's ignorance and instead fell into a deep sleep.

•   •   •   •

I woke a few hours later into the morning. The clock on the wall said six o'clock. Of course, the baby wasn't here yet. I stood up and stretched, looking around to see Jack still pacing. He looked at me when he saw me awake. "Do you think I'm allowed to pace the hallways?"

"Have you been awake this whole time?" I said in disbelief, yawning.

"No, I've been fast asleep," he quipped sarcastically, then said, "Of course! Who else would wake you when the news came?" But he had a smile on his face and good-natured tone to his words.

I yawned again. "Anything interesting happen since we arrived?"

"No. Dad's been by like ten times, though. Would you believe she's still in labor?"

I bit my lip against saying "duh" and instead said, "What else did he have to say?"

"Not much, actually. He kept saying how everything's going to be okay and to hang in there. Oh, and by the way, Ellie's picking us up at nine."

"Nice," I said. Stella was still sleeping soundly, and I let her sleep. Though I was still tired, I wasn't going to fall back asleep now. Besides, now that

Mom had been in labor for around four to five hours, it could happen at any time, and even if Jack woke me, I didn't want to be sleeping when Dad came with the news.

Fifteen minutes later, Dad entered the waiting room and smiled grimly at me. "Morning, sweetie."

"Morning." I went over and hugged him. "Anything on the baby?"

"Actually...yes. Jack, wake Stella, will you? I want to talk with you guys."

I got a sudden, horrible feeling. "Is everything all right?" I cried.

He didn't answer at first, then he said, "I think so, Faye."

After a few tries, Jack finally succeeded in waking Stella, who was very cranky as she stood up. "Why did you wake me? I was right in the middle of a good dream."

"Stel, cut it out. Baby news," Jack responded.

"Huh?" Stella rubbed her eyes and came over. "Hi, Daddy. How's Mom?"

"Kids." Dad addressed us all. "Listen. Everything is going to be all right, but there has been a complication with the delivery. The baby isn't breathing well enough. It was a very hard labor for your mother. She is okay, but the baby is in intensive care."

The news took a minute to sink in, then I felt dizzy, clutching the seat. "What?"

"Please don't worry about it. The doctors on staff here are very skilled. There really isn't anything to worry about." Dad seemed flustered, and he ran a hand through his hair.

Stella started to cry, and he comforted her. I didn't hear what he said.

The baby *was* a month early, I reminded myself. This kind of thing was probably very common for month-early babies. Right?

Jack spoke in a low voice. "Is it a boy or girl, Dad?"

Dad smiled for the first time, a real smile. "A boy," he said. "You've got a baby brother!"

The worry inside me temporarily evaporated, replaced by joy. A brother! *A baby brother!* I had a baby brother!

"What's his name?" I asked.

Dad smiled again. "Graham," he said. "Graham Thomas."

I felt a smile creep across my face.

"Graham," Jack repeated. "I have a brother." Then he said, "Is Mom alright?"

"Yes, Jack, she's alright." Dad stood up. "Do you want me to stay with you longer?"

"No," Jack said abruptly. "Go back to Mom."

"I'll be back soon," he promised, getting up. Seeing the nurse behind the desk, he said, "Bethany can answer your questions."

"Bethany?" Stella said.

But he had already left.

The nurse lifted a hand in a kind wave. "Hi. I'm Bethany."

Oh.

"You doing okay?" she asked us kindly, sounding concerned.

"Yeah," Jack said vaguely, and none of us said anything to the contrary.

Time dragged by. Before long I found I had to use the bathroom, and Bethany told me to go straight down the hallway and turn right. I got up and went in the designated direction, glad to be walking, to be up and out of the waiting room.

As I walked down the hall, a familiar voice caught my attention and I stopped in front of a room marked 213.

"I can't!" my mother wailed from inside the room. "I *can't*, Andrew! I can't lose another child. I can't, and I won't!"

I blinked, and stood stone-still outside the room. Then I took a step back, wondering if I'd really heard what I thought I'd heard.

Finally, coming to my senses, I continued walking, but my mind was elsewhere, all the what-if scenarios running through my head, scaring me and making me wonder if I had imagined it.

•   •   •   •

When I got back to the waiting room, Jack and Stella were gone. Bethany said they'd gone for a walk around the unit, and that made sense, though I did wish they'd waited so I could have gone along,

too. I sat down by myself in the room and stared at
the ceiling, thinking about what I'd heard and about
Graham and if he would make it. I wanted to shake
my head to clear the awful possibilities, but it
seemed there was nothing else on my mind to think
about. Every thought reminded me of little
Graham.

After what seemed like forever, but was
probably only five minutes, Bethany spoke again. I
looked up to find her sitting next to me. "You are
Faye Corcoran, right?"

"Yes," I said carefully.

"How are you doing?" she asked gently.

"Fine," I lied.

"You sure?"

"Yep," I said, acting uninterested. Why was
she bugging me? Why not leave me alone? Did she
not know I had a baby brother who was…in critical
care? That was what Dad said, right? The baby was
in critical care? Or maybe it was intensive. It made
no difference to me.

"If this is any assurance, I've seen this
situation with your brother before, and most of the
time, everything turns out just fine."

I felt a sarcastic comment pop up in my head.
Key word: Most…

"Well, thanks," I said bitterly.

She was silent.

Then she said, "I was looking at the files and
your name popped out to me." She paused before
continuing. "I used to work in the ER. I was

working there eight years ago, when they brought in a little girl who'd been in a car accident. A bad one. She was the same age as my little girl—she was five, I believe—and beat up really bad. Now I've seen my share of tragedies, but I will tell you, I'll never forget that time. I'll never forget you."

"Huh?"

"Honey, I was the nurse on staff when you were carried in after you had the car accident."

I had *not* been expecting that. I tried not to show it. "Um…okay?"

"No, really." She paused. "Do you remember that night?"

I shook my head slowly. "No."

"Oh, right, the amnesia. I'm sorry, of course you don't remember! I'm sorry."

"What, do you have amneeesia or something?" Suddenly Ellie's eyes grew wide. "That's it, Faye! I've figured out the mystery! You have amnesia!"

I blinked, suddenly alarmed, bringing myself back to the real world, but the scene in my mind remained, replaying itself over and over and over.

I looked back at the nurse. "Amnesia?"

"It's a condition where you lose your memory. In your case, it was pretty severe: the doctors doubted you'd remember anything before or during the accident, and they were right, I suppose. I'm sorry."

Amnesia? I knew what it was…but Mom had never once mentioned it when telling me about the wreck…yet, it made sense. Excepting my few dream-memory-things, I didn't remember much. But I *did* remember times before the accident. It wasn't as if I just blanked out on the whole first five years of my life...right? I wracked my brain for a specific memory to reassure myself, but the only thing that came to mind was the dream of snow.

Bethany interrupted my thoughts. "That was a horrible night. You should be thankful, really, that you don't remember it. Me, I'll never forget it. I still remember seeing you, right as they brought you in: you, your tousled, matted hair...that blood soaked pink and blue striped dress...You were missing a shoe. They said it came off in the impact." She stopped. "You don't know," she said after a long pause, "you don't know, what a very lucky girl you are, to have survived such an ordeal and to not even remember it..." Her eyes traveled to my scar. "Too lucky, really. Even in *that* accident, not everyone made it."

That one I *really* wasn't expecting.

"What?" I stammered.

Bethany looked at me gently. "I was told there was another mother and little girl..."

I felt numb; I sat there, unable to move, thoughts rushing through my brain. The accident I walked away from with only a scar... *killed* people? Another little child, another mother, both of their lives taken? But I had mine?

A thought whizzed through my brain. What if that was why Mom never talked about the accident? What if she had caused the accident? What if she felt guilty? That her and her daughter walked away while the other family lost a child and a mother?

"I'm really sorry, Faye." She seemed at a loss for words, and finally said, "I'm sure your little brother will be okay."

"Graham," I said. "His name's Graham."

"Graham, then." She stood up to leave. "I just wanted to make sure you were alright." Seeing my face, she added, "Oh, dear, maybe I shouldn't have even mentioned the accident. I'm sorry, sweetie. I'm sure your brother's gonna be okay. Do you have any other questions?"

Only a million.

"No," I said.

Stella and Jack walked back into the room. Stella was a little more perked up now from the walk, but Jack seemed as tired as ever. They came back and flopped in their seats.

"What time is Ellie picking us up again?" Stella asked.

I wracked my brain, but couldn't remember.

"Geez, Faye, what's wrong?" Jack asked.

"Nothing," I lied.

•　　•　　•　　•

The Andersons ended up picking us up about an hour later. The ride back was quiet, even with Ellie in the car. We stopped somewhere for breakfast, which was another somewhat silent event, and then arrived to Ellie's.

I'd had an uneasy feeling ever since Bethany's story, and the ride home only increased it for some reason.

I wanted to share with Ellie, but something was keeping me from it.

After a long day at Ellie's, I didn't even remember what we did, it was so hazy—we crawled into sleeping bags. Jack slept on the couch, and Stella slept with me and Ellie on the floor in Ellie's room. Stella was sound asleep within seconds, but I was awake, laying on my back and staring at the ceiling. Had it only been this morning we woke to Mom being in labor? Was it only today that we learned Graham might not make it? It all seemed like years ago.

Ellie, laying next to me, seemed to sense I was awake.

"It'll be okay, Faye," she said, softly, her voice penetrating the silence. "I promise."

Without even looking at her, I closed my eyes. "And how can you promise that? Are you in control of the situation? What if it's *not* okay?"

"Faye," she started, and then stopped. "I'm sorry."

"No, it's not your fault." I lay back down and resumed staring at the ceiling. "I'm sorry, Ellie. This whole thing has just gotten to me. I mean…I never would have guessed…you know…I never thought that…there would be a chance that he…."

"It's okay, Faye."

"Graham," I said. "His name's Graham."

"I know. I like it," she said softly. There was a brief silence, then she spoke again. "No matter what happens, Faye, it'll be alright. You know I'll always be here if you need me, right? Except when I'm at the doctor. If I'm at the doctor, then—"

"Ellie," I gently stopped her. "I'm not really in the mood for jokes."

She was silent. "You're my best friend, Faye. If your brother...doesn't make it, it affects me a lot too. But whatever the outcome, we'll get through this together. Alright?"

And then she was quiet, her hand still on my arm, and that was all I needed to know—that she was there.

•　　•　　•　　•

"Happy birthday to Faye!" they finish, clapping excitedly as I blew out all five candles on the cake. Wait, five?

"I thought I was turning thirteen," I say, and they all laugh at me. "Five is just big enough, dear."

"And I love your dress!" Brittney says, who is at my birthday celebration for whatever reason. I look down at my dress. It's blue and pink striped. As I continue to stare, something strange happens. The dress starts to look red. Bloody. I hold up my hand and see it bloody. I scream, and Brittney runs over and presses a cloth to my hand while Mom

looks over from a distance. Brittney runs a hand over my hair. "Don't worry, honey."

But I do worry. Suddenly I look at Mom and realize I don't recognize her. The woman holding the cloth looks unfamiliar, too. Where is my family? Where did everyone I know go?

"Do you have amnesia or something?" Mom says from across the table.

I woke sweaty and breathless. My dreams were getting worse and worse. Stranger and stranger. Creepier.

Ellie was still sleeping. I snaked out of my sleeping bag and walked downstairs, taking a seat at the counter. Mrs. Anderson smiled at me. "Morning, sweetie."

I returned the smile and bit into a forkful of the pancake I was offered.

Footsteps sounded on the stairs and Ellie appeared. She came and sat next to me.

"Are you okay?" she asked. "You've been acting weird since you got here."

Yeah, I know.

We finished breakfast, then went back upstairs. Stella woke when we walked in.

"Any news?" she asked.

When we shook our heads, she got up, grumbled, and went downstairs.

I flopped on my back on Ellie's bed and looked at the ceiling.

Then it poured out of me: about Graham and

about the nurse and the accident, and amnesia, and that there'd been deaths in the same accident I survived...even Mom's strange comment about losing another child, which had been bothering me consistently.

Ellie gaped at me. "Seriously? You *really* had amnesia?"

I nodded miserably.

She continued to stare. "How do you know the nurse is telling the truth? How can you trust her memory? Maybe *she* had amnesia."

"Ellie," I said. "She remembered every single detail about that night. Like, she even remembered my blue and pink striped dress I was wearing."

"Oh," Ellie said, then suddenly she looked at me, eyes large. Her jaw fell open. "Wait. *Blue and pink striped* dress?"

"I think so...why?"

Ellie looked at me, her expression one of shock. Slowly, she said, "Faye? That's the same dress Heather was wearing in the photograph."

chapter eighteen
heather ferry

A nauseating feeling swept over me; a wave of sudden familiarity as Ellie uttered the words. Something was connecting in my brain, like pieces of a puzzle sliding together, but I ignored it, pushing it aside as far as it would go. "What—what—do you mean?"

"I mean, Brittney's sister! Heather! The little girl who died in a car accident. That picture, remember, the one Brittney dropped? Heather was totally wearing a striped dress like that. I remember those pink, blue, and brown stripes as if I'd been there myself."

"No," I denied it. "She wasn't."

"Faye," she said in a low tone. "I memorized that picture."

"And...so what, then? If it is?"

"I don't know." She leapt up. "Let's look it up online. The Internet always has the answers." From the computer in Ellie's room, our eyes scanned the screen and the article Ellie had just clicked on. Ellie's voice, reading, drifted in and out of my understanding. Out of nowhere, chills raced up my spine as the words connected themselves before my eyes. Familiarity. Memory.

Heather Joy Ferry...born January 13...beloved daughter of Matthew Ferry ..survived by her older sister Brittney....remembered by her classmates...tragic end to a precious life....preceded in death by her mother, Pattijean Ferry....memorial service....

Familiarity...of Heather's life?

The puzzle pieces were forming a picture, one I hadn't wanted to create. The information rushed through my mind, ran before my eyes; there was no avoiding it, no pushing it aside.

I felt dizzy. Too dizzy...

"Faye," Ellie said in a tone like one I'd never heard. "You were in a car crash when you were five. Heather was also in a car crash when she was five. The day the accident happened, Heather was wearing a pink, blue and brown striped dress. When you arrived at the hospital after the accident, you were wearing a pink, blue and brown striped dress."

I stared at her. "What are you saying, Ellie?" My voice trembled.

Then all of a sudden my world was spinning.
The earth was spinning. All the words, all the
pictures, all the memories—finally snapping into
place. Not just from the article, not just about
Brittney...but everything. Anything I'd ever seen as
mysterious...everything about my life...all suddenly
made perfect sense.

Brittney.
The picture.
Heather being familiar.
The dress—
the same dress as Heather.
My dreams.
Snow on my birthday.
Memories of my accident.
The gingerdoodle Mom didn't remember.
My five-year-old self having green eyes.
The birthmark.
My scar.
The crash I'd been in.
My amnesia.
Amnesia!
Mom's comment on not losing another child.
My brown hair in a family of blondes.
My being blonde as a child.
The familiarity in the article.
Why Heather...
had been familiar...

Ellie's voice was barely a whisper.
"I'm saying you're Heather."

chapter nineteen
the real truth

I closed my eyes. Then I opened them and looked at Ellie. Her face was sullen.

"I'm Heather?"

She didn't say anything; she just stared at me. Then she leapt up and rushed out of the room, muttering something about having to tell her mom.

I sat in her room in disbelief. It couldn't be true. It couldn't. Yet...it *had* to be. What other explanation was there? Everything made sense now.

But it couldn't be true. How could it be true? If I really was Heather, then why had I grown up Faye? Why was I with the family that I was? How had it happened?

Part of me whispered to forget and just go home and pretend it never happened.

Then Brittney's face entered my mind.

Ellie came rushing back in, hysterical. "Faye! Faye! FAYE!"

Mrs. Anderson came in after, concerned. "Faye, is something wrong?"

Only everything.

"Momshesheatherandsheisheatherand—"

"Elisabeth Anderson, calm down!" her mom said sharply. "When you're speaking gibberish I can't understand you. Now, Faye, what's bothering you, honey?"

If I was Heather, who was Faye?

Mrs. Anderson spoke again, softer. "Faye, honey, tell me what's bothering you. Is it Graham? Are you worried about Graham, honey?"

"Mom. Mom. Mom, I told you," Ellie exclaimed, wringing her hands nervously. "Faye's Heather. And she's Heather and she remembers everything and—"

"Do I have to tell you again to calm down? And need I ask who this 'Heather' is?"

"Brittney's sister!" Ellie squeaked, biting her lip anxiously as her eyes flitted back and forth.

"Brittney?" her mom repeated.

"Their housekeeper!" Worry and confusion filled my friend's voice.

"Their housekeeper?" Mrs. Anderson arched an eyebrow. "Ellie, I don't have time for such nonsense. Calm down and speak once you're ready to communicate in normal English."

"But—Mom!" she cried. "Faye is Heather and Heather is Brittney's sister so that means Faye—I mean Heather—isn't a Corcoran—she's a Ferry!"

"Ellie, you're not helping anybody. Faye, talk to me, are you okay? Tell me what's bugging you. Did you get enough sleep last night?"

I remained speechless, just sat there numb.

"Are you feeling confused, sweetie? There's been a lot going on for you recently," she said gently.

I found words. "No," I managed. "I mean...I think Ellie's right."

That was all I could say. Mrs. Anderson looked at me kindly. "Well, whatever it is, honey, I'm sure it'll all be just fine."

"Brittney's last name is Ferry, Mom," Ellie hiccupped. "So Faye's is too. Her name's not even Faye, Mom! Faye! What can I call you? Mom—"

"Calm down, Ellie." Returning to me—"Faye, I'm not quite sure what's going on, but I'm positive that it'll all turn out just fine. It's been a hard time for your family and for you. When your parents pick you up, you guys can just figure this out at home. Does that sound okay?"

Her words blurred in my mind.

"I think I have amnesia," I said, a tear sliding down my cheek.

"What, sweetie?"

"Look, Mom." Ellie pointed to the computer. "See, look at this."

"Obituary for Heather..." Her mom stopped reading and looked at Ellie. "What is this, Elisabeth?"

"Faye remembers everything in this article." Ellie's voice was dangerously close to tears. "She remembers Heather's life, Mom!"

Mrs. Anderson bent over the computer.

Sudden emotions surged through me, and I started to cry. "How?" I said. "How is this possible? Someone's been lying to me. It's all fake. My whole life is a fake!"

"Don't say that, honey. I'm sure it'll all be figured out," Ellie's mom said, turning to look at me kindly. "How about I call your parents and you can talk it out? Everything is going to be just fine."

Everything won't be just fine, Mrs. Anderson, so stop saying that. I'm not Faye Corcoran. Someone's been lying to me my whole life. My very own parents have been deceiving me. I'm Heather Ferry. Not Faye Corcoran.

But somehow the words wouldn't make it past my lips. I only looked at her and half-nodded.

It couldn't be true.

Wait.

Did she say call my parents? She can't call my parents. If they even are my parents. I can't face them. They've lied to me. They've deceived me. Maybe they didn't know. Oh...I can't face them...!

I was crying now. Mrs. Anderson patted my hand soothingly. "It's all going to be just fine, Faye."

"Stay strong, Heather," Ellie whispered in my ear. Then she started to cry.

•   •   •   •

Later, I was told my parents had arrived. Numbly, I gathered my belongings and begged Ellie to let me stay longer.

"My mom's sure nothing is wrong," she whispered, horrified.

Mrs. Anderson said comfortingly, "Faye, really, it's all going to be fine. I'm sure you and your parents will get it this all figured out."

Stella was dancing around excitedly in the foyer, chanting something about Graham. Nearby, Jack leaned against the door with his hands in his pockets, muttering something about what a pain it was to not have his iPod. Both were clearly oblivious to my recent discovery.

I moved to stand near them, keeping my face neutral, trying to control the emotions threatening to emerge.

Jack noticed, of course. "Geez, what's wrong, Faye-Faye?"

His pet name didn't bother me today. If anything, it triggered more emotions.

Wait.

If I was Heather, then did that mean they weren't my siblings?

I swallowed twice. Blinked rapidly. Control the tears. Don't cry.

"Faye, what's up?" he said, swiping the bangs out of his eyes. "Come on, 'fess up. You can't fool your big brother."

I swallowed again. My mouth was dry. I croaked, "Nothing's wrong, Jack." Then swallowed again and looked away.

"What, think you can't trust your big brother?" he said sarcastically, then scoffed. "Suit yourself."

•   •   •   •

The short ride home was full of Stella's giggles.

If I was Heather, then did that mean this wasn't my family?

I found it getting harder to breathe. The car suddenly seemed claustrophobic. What if we got in another accident?

When we pulled into our driveway, all I could think of was getting to my bedroom, where I had privacy.

"Faye, where are you going?" Mom called, lightheartedly, as I headed towards the stairs. "Don't you want to hold your new brother?"

"What?" I looked back, and saw them, all together, all so familiar yet so unfamiliar: Mom, her long, blonde hair messy but still smooth, her eyes, despite the tiredness, still containing so much joy; the beautiful baby in her arms, all curled up in a blanket, so adorable; Dad, next to her, his eyes holding joy as well, a protective arm around my mother as he looked at me worriedly; Stella, sitting in a chair kicking her feet as she impatiently waited her turn to hold Graham, her blonde curls dancing and her eyes bright; and Jack, his hair in his eyes, slouched on the couch, his iPod out already, his eyes fixated on the screen as his fingers moved rapidly around.

Who were these people? Who was my family? Who was I?

"Nothing's wrong," I gasped, then turned and ran.

•　　•　　•　　•

Upstairs, I threw myself on my bed and cried, hugging the pillows to me. I didn't know how I'd ended up at the Corcorans', but it obviously wasn't how things were supposed to be. I was supposed to have grown up with Brittney. If I'd grown up with Brittney, I wouldn't have to know these people. Stella. Jack. Ellie?

A name returned to me.

Naomi Richter.

I blinked twice. I recognized that name. Not from the waterpark, but from *before*.

In the article. I'd seen her name. No, not in the article. In the comments or something. But I knew the name.

Naomi Richter—the girl I met at the waterpark?

Naomi Richter—the name of a girl who used to be my best friend?

Could they possibly be the same person?

I lay on my back and stared at the ceiling, eyes wide as memory upon memory of my previous best friend flooded my mind. Naomi. *Naomi.* Brown hair and cheery smile, a friend to run around in the backyard with, a friend to laugh with. The face in my memories was one of a cheerful five-year-old—a younger version of the girl I'd met at the waterpark. Sadness overwhelmed me as I remembered my friend from before the accident, then confusion as I thought of the friend at the waterpark. Could it even be possible that—

"Know what's funny? When we first met, you always used to call me Naomi." Ellie's words flooded back to me out of nowhere.

Chills crept up my spine. What were the chances...that Naomi, a girl I met once by chance, had, once upon a time, been my best friend?

Instead, my best friend is Ellie...but it was supposed to be Naomi.

What would my life have been like, had I always stayed with Brittney? Would I be laughing right now with Naomi, shivering at the thought of living without her, the same way I thought around Ellie? I missed Naomi, and suddenly all I wanted was to see her again.

Brittney—*suddenly I remembered Brittney:* the older, sisterly figure who read to me, played with me, hugged me, been there for me...who could have done this to me? Hatred seeped into me towards the person responsible. How could anyone do this? How could anyone have done this to me…to put me in a life that wasn't mine and steal me from the people who loved me most?

My mother!—

I remembered my mother, and suddenly my breath caught as memories flooded me, memories of her kind face and soft words, loving embrace— of her love. Of the gingerdoodle. I gasped. The *gingerdoodle*! That had been my true mother I made them with—not Mom! That was why Mom didn't remember! Eyes wide, I stumbled to the window and pressed a palm to it. *My* mom was killed in the car accident. *My* mother. *My mother*, the one I'd only just discovered…gone? The one I'd baked gingerdoodles with? It felt like I'd only just met her, only just realized my love for her, and now, knowing she was gone sent another crash of strange emotions on me.

I wanted my mom more than anything else, and that was the one thing I couldn't have.

An image of a room, one that had probably once been mine, appeared in my brain: a room on the small side, painted a pale, lavender color. A white little-girl bed and white desk, and small walk-in closet where I hid all the time from Brittney or Naomi during endless games of hide-and-seek.

Where had those happy days gone? How had I ended up here? Why was I here? What was happening to my life?

chapter twenty
brittney ferry

A knock on the door interrupted my thoughts. I panicked and frantically rushed to wipe my eyes with my sleeve to hide the tears. "Who is it?"

"Faye, honey?" The door opened and Dad stepped in, looking worried. I turned around and hiccupped. "Yes?"

He came over and sat next to me. "Faye, I got a call from Mrs. Anderson."

I frowned. Why—*oh*! She would be calling to tell him—that I thought—

"W-What'd she say?"

"Sweetie, I just want to let you know everything is fine. Nothing is wrong at all. I don't know what got into you back at Ellie's, but you are my daughter. Why don't you tell me what you're worried about, and we can talk it out? I don't want you to ever feel like you don't belong."

My heart thumped in my chest. His words reassured me. Maybe it all *was* just my imagination.

But then what about Brittney? And Heather? And everything we'd discovered?

If I was Heather, than did this mean this wasn't my father?

How?

How could such a thing even be possible?

How could such a thing even happen?

How *had* it happened?

Why was I here?

Why

was

I

here?

He sat across from me, his eyes keeping comforting contact with mine.

I took a deep breath. "When's Brittney coming back?" Maybe if I just saw Brittney, everything would magically slide into place. At any rate, if it was true, Brittney would know what to do. She had to.

"Honey, here's the thing. Brittney was mostly here to help around the house during your mother's pregnancy. Now that Graham's here, we've decided we are no longer in need of Brittney's services."

I stared at him in disbelief. No. He wasn't suggesting that...

"Brittney isn't coming back, Faye."

I couldn't speak for fear. If it was true—how would it ever be figured out? How could I ever be—how could anything—how could it be settled—if Brittney wasn't here?

"I—I need to call Ellie," I stammered out, feeling faint.

"That's the other thing I wanted to talk to you about, sweetheart," he said, gently. "Your mother and I have been talking, especially after this whole thing at Ellie's house. We've decided you are going to need to take a break from Ellie for a little bit. Get out and make some new friends. We're not liking Ellie's influence on you."

This was not happening.

No. This could not be happening.

Ellie was the one who helped me realize the truth.

And that's why they're banning you from it, my inner self told me.

My world was dizzy again.

Dad patted my back affectionately. "Come down when you're ready, honey. Our family's not complete without you." He left. I sat on my bed, my world spinning again. That. *That* was the final straw. No Brittney…no Ellie…no…*no*…this was all wrong. All wrong. Everything was wrong. I was wrong. How could I be right if I wasn't even Faye? I wasn't Faye. I was Heather. How could I be Heather? Everything was wrong. Nothing was okay anymore. I couldn't handle it. I needed answers.

•   •   •   •   •

I walked down the stairs one step at a time, carefully and steadily. *Keep your expression straight.*

Stella grinned like nothing else, cradling Graham in her arms. When she saw me, her smile widened. "Look, Faye, I have Graham!"

"I see, Stella." I kept my voice even as stepped into the room, towards her and the rest of people I had called my family.

She scrunched up her nose. "What's wrong?"

I gathered what courage I had. "Mom?"

She looked at me, her face blissful. "What, honey?"

I swallowed hard, standing there in front of them, feeling immediately isolated. I blinked and cleared my throat, trying to summon the words I so desperately needed.

"I'm not Faye?"

It came out as a timid question.

The house became horribly silent.

I felt all eyes on me. In Stella's arms, Graham squirmed and made a small whimper.

"I'm not Faye." My voice was barely a whisper, but it came out stronger this time; more confidently. My gaze wavered, then I found Mom. "Am I?"

Mom's happiness faded, and her face paled as she looked at me.

I clenched my fists at my sides, my hands

sweaty. Then I spoke the words I'd been longing to speak ever since the discovery.

"What happened?"

Mom's expression was one of utter hopelessness; Dad stepped in, his voice warningly. "Faye, I thought we already talked about this. Everything's just fine."

"No. It's not." I was having trouble controlling my emotions. "Everything's not fine. I'm not Faye. Am I, Mom?"

She stared at me, her eyes full of despair and at the same time so much longing. Her eyes glistened with tears.

"What else was a woman expected to do?" she whispered.

I stared at her.

"Kimberly," Dad interjected, and my gaze darted to him as my instinct instantly told me something wasn't right. His voice took on an unnatural tone, deep and throaty. "I had this under control."

I stared at him for a minute before an unforeseen terror overcame me as I looked breathlessly at a man who I no longer recognized. I stood, petrified.

Then I ran.

I dashed through the walls of someone else's house to the front door, ignoring the voices calling out to me using someone else's name. I ran out the door and down the driveway—down the sidewalk— to the only place I could think of to go.

I flew down the street, running faster than I'd ever run before. Tears stung my eyes as I ran.

I reached Ellie's and began desperately ringing the doorbell. Ellie opened it, her forehead creased, and she screamed, "Faye! What are you doing here?"

Breathless, I told her; explained about Dad firing Brittney and saying I couldn't hang out with Ellie anymore; how I tried to tell them I wasn't Faye and how they reacted.

"I couldn't handle it anymore," I sobbed.

"Faye!" She hugged me tightly. "Oh, Faye, Faye, Faye!"

Mrs. Anderson appeared. "Faye?"

"Mom, it was the truth," cried Ellie, tears in her eyes now as well. "It was all the truth!"

"What was, sweetie?"

"Faye being—Heather."

Mrs. Anderson slowly looked from me to her daughter.

"It's true," I said, still sobbing and feeling dizzy. "It's all true. Please help me. I can't go back!"

A worried expression on her face, she ushered us inside, where I collapsed on the floor—the room spinning around me. She shut the door carefully and then said, "Would either of you like to fully explain to me what's going on?"

"Everything I told you earlier," Ellie croaked. "About Faye being Heather and being Brittney's sister. It's all true."

"Please don't send me back there," I begged.

"I'm too afraid."

"Afraid?" Ellie said.

"I—I don't know how to explain it," I stuttered. "I just—at the end—I was talking—and he spoke—and—"

"It creeped you out," Ellie whispered, reading my mind exactly. I nodded wordlessly and continued to cry. "I mean, I—I don't even know who they *are* anymore!"

Mrs. Anderson left the room. Ellie followed her and then came back a couple minutes later. "She tried calling your home, but nobody answered."

I just sat there and cried.

Crying was becoming exhausting.

A phone rang a few minutes later. Mrs. Anderson called, "Ellie!"

Ellie got up, and then returned a little bit later. "Faye, Jack called."

"What'd he say?" I hiccupped.

Ellie didn't answer. Instead, I turned and found Mrs. Anderson at my side, soothingly rubbing my back.

"It's okay, Faye. I was able to talk to your brother, and you aren't going to go home anytime soon." Her tone was flustered, and one look told me she was overwhelmed with sudden responsibility. "You'll have to stay here while we figure it out. Jack—"

I interrupted. "You—you know?"

"I know," she said gently. "Now listen. Your brother called me to tell me some things. Faye, your mom took off with Graham, and your dad went after her. Jack said that they think you've lost your mind and Stella's really scared, so I told them to just come down, here. Is that okay?"

I sunk to my knees again, her words rolling over and over in my mind. Stella? Jack? Here?

"What can we do?" I whispered.

"About what, sweetie?"

"About *me*!" I exclaimed. "How are we going to get this figured out? I'm not going back. I can't live a lie anymore..." I buried my face in my knees.

"Brittney."

Brittney?

At the word, hope filled me and I looked up to find Ellie staring at me. "Brittney," she said again.

"Brittney," I repeated, and I leapt to my feet, hope restored for the moment. "Brittney! She'll know what to do!"

"And I have the flyer upstairs!" Ellie exclaimed, eyes wide, and she took off upstairs, appearing a minute later with the green paper. I didn't even wonder how she had gotten ahold of it; all I could think of was the number that was printed at the bottom of the paper, and how, by calling it, my life would be forever altered.

•   •   •   •

The doorbell rang seemingly moments later. *Brittney!* My heart leapt in my chest, but it sunk a moment later when Ellie called, "Mom, Jack and Stella are here."

Jack and Stella barged in, worry filling their eyes. Jack saw me and exclaimed, "I knew it! You haven't lost your mind after all."

"Knew what?" Stella asked.

"Faye." He turned away.

"That doesn't even make any sense, Jackson!" Stella cried as they walked into the family room, leaving me on my own in the front room. Well, not completely alone. Ellie never moved from my side.

I heard Mrs. Anderson talking in soft, gentle tones to Jack and Stella, presumably trying to explain in the mildest way possible what was going on.

"Told ya," I heard Jack yell. Stella's whiny, desperate-sounding voice overruled his yells as she struggled to comprehend the situation. "But why?"

"We don't know quite yet, honey," I heard Mrs. Anderson respond, flustered. "Just sit quietly with your brother until we figure this out. It's all gonna be fine."

"Eh?" I heard Jack again. "And I'm sure that's the same thing you told Faye. And look—would you call this situation fine?"

With Jack's last comment, I found it safer to tune them out, burying my head in the couch pillows.

●   ●   ●   ●

Ten minutes later, Ellie nudged me. "Faye, Brittney's here." Her voice was quiet.

I looked up and wiped my eyes. "Here? Now?"

"In the driveway."

I stood up and went to wait by the door, peering outside to see Brittney exuberantly slamming her car door before striding up the path, her face tense.

I crept back from the window, suddenly afraid, but Ellie was there. "Stay strong, Heather," she whispered for the second time, only this time didn't follow with a round of tears. I clenched her hand tightly, and she squeezed back, trying to encourage me despite her own pain.

Mrs. Anderson appeared, it seemed, out of nowhere to open the door. Brittney's eyes alighted on me, and I felt her taking me in, slowly. I finally turned my face, and our eyes met. For the first time I truly noticed her eyes—pale but vibrant blue. Exactly like my own. Her caramel hair, so close to my shade of brown. Looking at her, I suddenly saw myself in her. My very thoughts seemed to tremble. She was my sister.

"Heather," she finally whispered.

Mrs. Anderson cleared her throat. "Brittney," she said, her voice level, "is Faye—is she your sister?"

Brittney slowly looked from her to Ellie, to Stella in the doorway, then finally to me.

"Yes," she said. "Heather is my sister."

Then suddenly I was enveloped in her embrace, and felt her sobs shake her body as she squeezed me to her. And that was all it took, that feeling—that oh-so-familiar feeling—of security that I got from her arms wrapped around me, that was all it took—to know it was true. Tears poured down my cheeks as we clung to one another, tears of happiness and of sadness, of joy and of sorrow. I let her embrace me, crying with her over all what was lost, and what was gained.

After only a few minutes that felt like hours, she pulled away and looked at me lovingly. "I've missed you so much, Heather," she said, awed. "I can't believe this. I mean, I do, but I don't..."

"I find this rather hard to believe as well...Brittney." I looked up to see Mrs. Anderson looking at us, concerned painted on her face. "Would you mind explaining, Brittney, honey, how this came to be, and how Faye is your sister? And why she was living with this family—that wasn't hers?"

Brittney looked at me, her eyes full of love, and then back at Mrs. Anderson. "Yes," she said. "Most of it, anyway. Can we sit down somewhere? This is shocking. I mean, I've known for a while this—that she's Heather...but the reality has only just hit me."

We went into the front room. I followed along robotically; Brittney's arm remained on my shoulders. I didn't want to have this conversation. I wanted to wake up right now, in my bed, in my house, have it all be a dream…*I wanted to be Faye again.*

But at the same time…I didn't. There was an element of peace. A sense of security. A sense of truth—and everything felt…right. Despite my fears and worries, I knew Brittney was right when she said I was Heather. I sat down next to Brittney on the couch, and then I had the sudden urge to lean my head on her shoulder, the same way I did when I was five, so I did. She was my sister, after all. She squeezed me, and I closed my eyes. Never had anything felt so right.

Ellie sat down next to me and took my hand. Her hand was sweaty and she squeezed mine a bit too tightly. I didn't say anything.

Brittney took a shuddering breath, and began. "Years ago," she said, "my mother and—Heather were in a car accident. It was awful." She paused. "They told me my mom died, and I believed that. That was so hard, to be fourteen years old and without a mother. But then they told me that Heather, my sweet five-year-old sister, was dead as well, and that…that I couldn't believe. I refused to believe it, actually. Heather couldn't be dead. I read about the girl who'd survived, and I just…knew…" She took a breath and went on. "I knew my sister, and the girl who they said had died—I still don't know who that was, but all I knew was that it wasn't you."

Mrs. Anderson cut in. "Brittney, you've been referring to two girls here. One of them is Heather, but who's the other, and what does she have to do with any of this?"

Brittney shifted uncomfortably. "I—I don't know, exactly. See, the thing is, the accident my mother and Heather were in—it was a collision...and in the other car, there was another mother and child, a little girl the same age as Heather. They said she had survived, and Heather had died...but I didn't believe it..."

There was a moment of silence. I opened my eyes and saw Jack and Stella had entered the room. Jack was leaning against the doorframe, his eyes vacant. Stella's lower lip was trembling as she listened, and her eyes pooled with tears. "Faye? Does this mean you're not my big sister?"

Brittney looked sympathetically at Stella. "Stella, Jack, I'm really sorry...for you to have to...go through this." She took a deep breath. "But Faye isn't Faye Corcoran," she said softly.

"She's my sister, Heather Ferry."

chapter twenty-one

imposter

"It was so hard," Brittney continued. "I was the one and only person who thought like this. How many times I tried to tell Dad...my father...what I thought, but he always dismissed it. Didn't even consider that it was a possibility..."

"Who was it?" Mrs. Anderson asked, speaking my thoughts exactly. "Who died, if Faye...Heather...didn't?"

"I don't know." Brittney looked at me briefly.

"It's as if they were switched," Mrs. Anderson said softly, thinking out loud. "Heather...and the other girl. Because everyone thought Heather was dead—"

"—and the other girl was alive." Brittney shifted positions, and I sat up, wiping hair from my eyes. She looked at me, and suddenly I felt all eyes on me.

"Are you saying…" I struggled for words. "Are you saying…there's some other girl named Faye, who died…and then everyone was tricked into thinking it was Heather who died…and then tricked me into thinking I was Faye?"

Silence ensued.

"Switched," Jack murmured. "Of course switched," he said. "No! It can't be."

All eyes darted to him.

"If they were switched, then my sister's dead," he said. "Are you telling me I've been living with a fake my whole life? And I was tricked into thinking she was my sister?"

"You? What about me?" Stella hollered.

"You're different," he snapped. "Whoever did this…to me…and Faye…is going to have me to deal with!"

"Jack," said Brittney suddenly. "It had to have happened during the accident. If one girl's gone and the other mother is, it could be really easy for the surviving mother to…" She trailed off.

I stared at her. "No," I said. "You're not saying…"

"You were kidnapped, Faye." Jack crossed his arms and laughed bitterly. "Mom kidnapped you. Faye died, so she just had to take Heather. Don't know why I haven't figured it out by now." The way he said it suggested he was doing his best to cover his emotions.

Everything was so hazy and confusing.

"Alright," Mrs. Anderson said. "I think I'm following so far. But there's no way the police would have missed all this. I mean, two completely different girls are switched! They'd have to have someone identify the bodies."

Brittney seemed uncomfortable. "My father *did* identify the bodies," she said. "But he got it wrong."

"Well, I could see that. But how about DNA testing?"

"Mrs. Anderson, it was a car accident, and the bodies were nearly unrecognizable. I don't think there was any need for a DNA test. I mean—there *was* need for one, we know that now, but they wouldn't know that then."

Mrs. Anderson nodded. "But how did you come to be at Faye's house? I mean, what are the chances that the one house—"

"Mrs. Anderson, it wasn't chance," Brittney interrupted. "It's a long story, but basically, I tracked down the family that took Heather. There was a college not far from here I wanted to attend, so I used it as an excuse to temporarily move here. I thought that maybe if I saw you, I'd know. Then one day, I did see you—at the grocery store, with your mom. You were probably eight or nine years old, and I knew it was you instantly. That was when I knew just seeing you wasn't going to be enough, to make everything fix itself. I started looking for ways to go further…then a few years later I saw your— uh—mom at the library and overheard her talking about how messy her house was these days, with all her kids and such. So I came up with the idea for a cleaning service. I thought that if I could just get into the house...I could see you...try to make things right." She smiled. "And then I started at your house, and you know the rest."

"No, I don't," I said, sitting up. "Why didn't you...talk to me...or something, right away?"

"I knew within a month of my job that I'd found my sister, but I just didn't know what to do. I wanted to call the police, but I was afraid you weren't going to remember me and it'd turn into some huge mess. I just...waited, in hope, that just by being there constantly it would trigger some memory and you'd remember me. Then yesterday...I was told I was no longer needed at your house and I thought my life was over. How could I live, knowing you were right there, I was in your house, and I didn't even find a way to tell you anything?" She smiled. "Then I got your call."

I let her story completely sink in, and was left speechless. Brittney cared that much about me...she loved me that much...to spend the last eight years since the accident doing everything in her power to find me. And even when she had me, she waited, to made sure I remembered and wasn't afraid...despite all her despair in needing me back.

"I'm so glad you found me," I whispered.

"I can't live without you now, Heather," she responded.

Heather. A foreign name. A name of a girl who died. A name of Brittney's sister...My name?

"What now?" Mrs. Anderson asked.

"Well, Mrs. Anderson, I can't live without Heather anymore. No matter what we do, I need to be with Heather."

Heather.

Heather.

"Who's Faye, then?" I asked, my voice muffled.

"I can answer that." Jack's voice was gruff. "Faye's the name of my sister. Who died in a car wreck. Who I barely remember. Who you replaced." His voice was tight. "I lost my sister. Who is Faye? I don't even remember her personality. Was she quiet? Outspoken? All that's left in my mind as 'Faye' is the image of you..."

I ran. Jumped up from the couch. Raced through the house to the only place I could think of to go: Ellie's bedroom. I ran away from everything...away from reality...away from the truth and collapsed on Ellie's bed.

•   •   •   •

I didn't realize I'd shut the door, but when I looked up, someone was knocking. Then Brittney came in and quietly sat beside me on the bed, smoothing my hair as I sat there motionless, unable to even cry.

"Heather?" she said. "It's gonna be okay."

"No!" I cried. "I'm not okay. Everything and

everyone that I know has been untrue. Even my identity is false!"

"It's okay," she whispered, clutching me to her. Then she said, "It's gonna be hard, but we're going to get through this together. Alright?"

Her words comforted me, and I sniffled. "Will I ever see Ellie again?" I whispered. "Or Stella? Jack? Logan? Graham?"

Brittney didn't answer right away. Then she said, "We'll make a way, sweetie. We'll make a way."

"What about—Mom and Dad?"

"I don't know, honey. I just don't know."

We sat together for a while, silent, her arm encircling me. "We'll make a way, Heather," she whispered. "We'll make a way. We'll get through this together."

After a little bit longer, she said, "Why don't you come downstairs?"

I nodded wordlessly and followed her, feeling so much better.

chapter twenty-two
saying goodbye to faye

The last time I saw my siblings before I left, I was at Ellie's house preparing to leave. Mrs. Anderson was figuring out the legal situation, but I paid little attention to all of that. Brittney told me all I needed to know, and I had no desire to know all the legal issues. All I knew was Brittney was my sister.

Brittney had told me that today we were going to the Child and Family Protective Services office to finalize things. I would say goodbye to Mom and Dad at the office—a neutral zone, Brittney explained, with a social worker and lawyers nearby to make sure everything was fine—but Stella and Jack were coming by Ellie's, instead, to say goodbye. Brittney told me that my parents probably wouldn't put up a fight about the whole thing, so it should be a semi-peaceful ordeal, even if it was going to be the most difficult thing I'd ever do.

It'd been a few days since the discovery. I was still struggling, but I was getting better. Brittney had been a constant encouragement, reminding me who I was whenever I doubted it. I chose to stay at Ellie's. Stella and Jack had returned home after the first night, and then gone home once they found Mom.

I walked down the stairs that day that Stella and Jack had come and found Stella, sitting on the window seat, stiff and still, her finger playing with a loose thread as she stared out the window, her eyes absent.

I stood there for a moment and watched her. She made no movement. I had never seen my sister so quiet, so still. Obviously she knew what was going on, but I'd never thought it would have affected her so deeply.

I walked over, swallowing tears, and sat on the bench next to her. She gave no response.

Her curly, blonde hair fell gently down, past her face, and her eyes remained absent. I reached out after a minute and stroked her hair, smoothing it behind her ear. This normally annoyed her; today she didn't make any motion of annoyance, didn't give any response whatsoever.

"Stella?" I said, gently.

"What?" she mumbled.

"Stella…" My voice caught, and I choked back tears desperately.

Suddenly she turned to me wildly. "Faye, I swear, every time I was annoying or irritating or anything, I promise, I didn't mean it! I really didn't! I didn't! You're the best sister ever and you can't just leave!" She collapsed in tears, throwing her arms around my neck and sobbing into my shoulder.

I squeezed her back, sudden tears streaming down my cheeks as I clutched my little sister, never wanting to let go. "Stella, I promise, I never meant a word of it, either. I couldn't ask for a better little sister."

She squeezed me and I squeezed her tightly, holding her in my arms as we cried. I could never let go. She was my sister. I didn't care if she'd been annoying in the past. All I wanted now was to hear her laugh, to see her scowl as she yelled at me. Anything but this miserable little girl in my arms.

She eventually pulled away, her face wet and eyes puffy. She sniffled and wiped her eyes, then leaned her head back on my chest. "I'm still gonna see you, right?"

"Of course," I whispered. "We'll make a way."
She nodded. I hugged her to me.
"Promise?" she said.
"I promise," I said.
"And we'll write, and email, and text, and FaceTime—"
"Stella," I said. "You're my sister. I don't care if you aren't biologically. In my heart, you're always going to be little sister. I don't care if I have to drive

five hundred miles to see you, we're not losing touch. I promise."

She sniffled again, and then nodded.

"Stella?" My voice was barely audible.

"What?"

"I love you," I choked out, then I just sat there, holding her to me so tightly and wishing I could stay like this forever.

Jack appeared a little while later. I didn't notice his appearance until I felt his arms around me. I was still holding Stella, though by the way she sat quietly I thought she might have fallen asleep in my arms. I didn't care; I simply hugged her tighter. I looked up to see Jack, my big brother who brags he never cries, looking at me with tears dripping down his cheeks.

Stella shifted in my arms, and I squeezed her so tightly as Jack squeezed me the same way, and in that way we all sat there and cried.

We calmed down a bit after a while, but remained sitting there silently. I heard Mrs. Anderson talking in the background to Brittney about Faye.

Faye.

I knew who Faye was now, too. Brittney found that out, later. Faye was the real child of my so-called parents. She had died in the accident that killed my true mother, so Faye's mom took me and said I was Faye, then said Faye was Heather. I'd been kidnapped. The thought still made my heart pound and breath catch, but it was getting better

and the thought wasn't as intense as it was the first time I found out.

The mystery behind my memory of snow was solved, too, and the answer had shocked me. July twenty-third wasn't my birthday; it was Faye's. My birthday was January thirteenth. I was a full six months older than I had always believed. When I was laughing and swimming at the pool that day, it hadn't even been my birthday. I'd already been thirteen for a long time—in fact, I was older than Ellie.

In contrast to everything else going on, this was minor; but to me, it was yet another false aspect of my life, that even my birthday wasn't even mine anymore, but that of the girl I replaced.

"They were switched," Mrs. Anderson murmured from across the room as Brittney finished explaining. "As if Kimberly simply said to Heather, 'You'll be like Faye,' then made it her reality."

"Exactly," Brittney said, her voice somber. "Heather would be Faye, in her mind, then."

"But...Mom." Ellie's voice interrupted the conversation, timid and quiet. "Why would Mrs. Corcoran do...why would she do that?"

I heard Mrs. Anderson's sigh. "Well, honey...sometimes, in the midst of a tragedy, people do strange things; they can't think right. I don't know what I'd do, if I ever lost you. She must have been...well...just so traumatized—she must have felt like she had to do something about it. And probably in the chaos of that accident, it *seemed* like the right choice. That's why it's so important to always do the right thing, no matter what you're facing. Otherwise...things end up like...this."

"Faye?" Jack said, his voice stiff. I looked up through teary eyes. "Jack?"

"Faye? I...I'm gonna miss you."

It was the closest thing of adoration I'd ever received from my tough older brother. I looked at him sadly. "I'm going to miss everybody, Jack...you, Stella, Ellie, Graham..." My voice broke off.

"Faye," he said, his voice a bit stronger as he searched for words. Finally he gave up and said, "Keep in touch...please. Don't forget us, and we won't forget you...Heather."

"Oh, Jack." I stood up and placed a sleeping Stella on the seat before turning and hugging my brother. He hugged me back for probably the first time, his arms encircling me.

Finally he tore away. "Seriously, though. Keep in touch. Promise?"

I swallowed, and nodded. "Promise."

He nodded at me in return, then disappeared, muttering something about having to use the bathroom.

I watched him go, the tears in my eyes no longer ones of sadness. I filled my thoughts with ones of Brittney and of Naomi and of my true family, then made a silent vow to never, ever, forget Faye or any of her family. To never forget about Ellie, Logan, Jack, Stella, and Graham. I would keep in touch. I had to.

Stella was sleeping peacefully and I went over and gently kissed her forehead. Faye's life was over. It had taken her eight years to die, but now she was truly gone. And while I missed her so dreadfully, I also knew who I was—Heather Ferry—and that I was done playing the part of someone else.

I didn't know what lay ahead of me. I didn't know exactly what was coming next, or what I'd have to face in the near future. But right now, those things didn't matter. I knew Brittney was my sister, I knew the truth, and most importantly, I knew who I was.

And that was really all that mattered.

Gingerdoodles

INGREDIENTS

GINGERSNAP COOKIE DOUGH:

1 cup packed brown sugar

¾ cup shortening

¼ cup molasses

1 egg

2 ¼ cup all-purpose flour

2 teaspoons baking soda

1 teaspoon ground cinnamon

1 teaspoon ground ginger

½ teaspoon ground cloves

¼ teaspoon salt

SNICKERDOODLE COOKIE DOUGH:

¾ cup granulated sugar

½ cup butter, softened

1 egg

¾ cup plus 1 teaspoon all-purpose flour

½ cup whole wheat flour

1 teaspoon cream of tartar

½ teaspoon baking soda

½ teaspoon salt

CINNAMON-SUGAR:

¼ cup granulated sugar

2 teaspoons ground cinnamon

DIRECTIONS

1. Heat oven to 375 F. Line cookie sheet with cooking parchment paper.
2. In a large bowl, mix brown sugar, shortening, molasses and egg. Stir in remaining Gingersnap Cookie Dough ingredients.
3. In another large bowl, beat ¾ cup sugar, the butter and eggs with an electric mixer on medium speed until well mixed. Stir in remaining Snickerdoodle Cookie Dough ingredients.
4. For each cookie, shape a level teaspoon of Gingersnap cookie dough and a rounded teaspoon of Snickerdoodle Cookie Dough into a ball. In a small bowl, mix ¼ cup sugar and 2 teaspoons cinnamon. Roll dough balls in cinnamon sugar; place on cookie sheet.
5. Bake 9 to 11 minutes or until light golden brown around edges. Cool 2 minutes on cookie sheet. Remove to cooling rack to cool completely.

Acknowledgements

To start, I thank my Lord Jesus Christ. He is the one who has given me such a passion for writing, and for that I can never be thankful enough.

Thank you to my wonderful family and friends; to my parents for their hours spent editing and formatting, both with this book and the last. To my editors, Matt Ingle and Ellie Holcomb, thank you for taking time to read this book and helping me become a better writer. Iain MacKinnon, thank you for sharing your expertise in graphics and web design, you rock! To Angelica Fernandez, my incredible illustrator; your imaginative artwork truly captured the characters and scenes. Fantastic job! Thank you Marissa, Emily, and my friends and leaders at church and co-op; you all are a constant encouragement. To the staff at my local library, thank you so much for your support. And thank you Avery and Kinley!

And finally thank you to all my readers—you all are awesome!

ABOUT THE AUTHOR

J.C. Buchanan is 14 years old and has been homeschooled her entire life. She has been writing and reading for as long as she can remember, and hopes to pursue a lifelong career in writing. Besides writing, she enjoys reading, hanging out with friends, babysitting, volunteering at church, and making movies. J.C. lives in Illinois with her mom, dad, and three younger brothers. She has written two books: *The Hidden Amethyst* (2013) and *You'll Be Like Faye* (2015). To find out more or to contact J.C., please visit her website: **jcbuchanan.com**

Made in the USA
Monee, IL
11 May 2025